MOVING IN

MOVING IN

BY ALFRED SLOTE

J. B. LIPPINCOTT   NEW YORK

Moving In

Library of Congress Cataloging-in-Publication Data
Slote, Alfred.
Moving in.

Summary: Eleven-year-old Robby and his thirteen-
year-old sister, Peggy, involve themselves in some
elaborate schemes to discourage their widowed father's
budding romance and to persuade him to move back to
their old hometown.
[1. Moving, Household—Fiction.   2. Fathers—
Fiction] I. Title.
PZ7.S635Mo 1988   [Fic]   87-45569
ISBN 0-397-32261-5
ISBN 0-397-32262-3 (lib. bdg.)

To Elaine Cousins, Bill Wrobleski,
Marty Walker, and Jonathon Niemczak,
who led me through the electronic
jungle.

MOVING IN

There was no way I wanted to move to Arborville, Michigan. All my friends lived in Massachusetts. Before we moved to Massachusetts we'd lived in California, and that move had been hard enough. I couldn't go through it again, and I told Dad that.

"I'm not moving," I announced at the table one night.

My sister, Peggy, who's thirteen, two years older than me, thought that was very funny.

"So you're going to stay here in Watertown? Who are you going to live with? Monk Kelly?"

She was picking on my best friend. Peggy didn't like any of my friends. Which was okay, since I didn't like any of hers.

Dad told us to stop nattering. He told me he was truly sorry about this move because he could remember how he had been moved around as a kid. Grampa Miller had been an army colonel, and Dad hadn't gone to the same school two years in a row. As a kid he'd lived in Texas, California, Illinois, Oklahoma,

Florida, Pennsylvania, Georgia, Alabama . . . you could practically name them all. "It was one of the reasons I didn't want an army career," he told us.

I believed that Dad believed that, but it would be hard to picture him as an army officer in the first place. He's so quiet. He hardly ever raises his voice, even when he's angry. He'll laugh from time to time, especially at me. But he's definitely not the outgoing type. He keeps everything inside him. He never sings, hums, he never whistles. Though Mom said Dad had whistled when he courted her.

Dad's an electronics engineer. He met Mom at college, where she was a writer on the student newspaper, and they got married."Opposites attract," Dad said, and I guess they did.

They started moving right away in Dad's career. They moved to New York State, where Dad worked for IBM, and then to California, where Dad worked for a bunch of little companies and where me and Peggy were born. All we did after that, it seems to me, was move. I once told Dad he could've been a general in the army for all the moves he was making.

Since I could remember, we moved from Silicon Valley, California, where I was born, to Massachusetts. Which doesn't sound like a lot, I know, but you got to understand every big move means a lot of little moves. You never get to the right house right away. For instance, when we moved to Massachusetts we lived in Malden first and then in Scituate and then in Brookline and finally in Watertown, which didn't look like such a hot town but we had a great little house and I had great friends like Monk Kelly. You don't make a friend like Monk every day. Watertown was even good for Dad. It was near the company he worked for—Photonics. Even Peggy liked Watertown, and she doesn't usually like anywhere. All in all it was a great place to live, and now Dad said we were going to move again.

"You know," I said to him, "you're a great problem in our lives."

Dad laughed. "I guess I am. Let's hope that when you get married, Robby, you won't be a problem to your kids."

"Who'd want to marry him?" Peggy said, unable to resist an opening when she should have, because it was important that we present a united front against Dad. But that's how older sisters are. They always have to get their jabs in. That ended any serious talk about not moving. Not that it would have changed anything. Kids have nothing to say about what happens to them. And that's the beginning and end of that.

That night I went over to Monk Kelly's house and told him what was happening.

"You going back to California?"

"No. You won't believe this. Michigan."

"Michigan? That's cold, man."

"Tell me about it."

"If you think *we* get snow. I mean, you're gonna be *buried* under the white stuff."

"C'mon, Monk, I don't wanna talk about it."

"They got good hockey there though. Michigan, Minnesota, and Massachusetts. The three M's. Ever think about that?"

"No."

Monk was trying to cheer me up, and maybe himself, too, but it wasn't working, because after a while he was silent, and then he said, "What are we going to do for a shortstop?"

"I don't know. But you got all winter to think about it."

"Heck, Robby, we'll miss you even more in hockey. You think they got hockey teams in this town that you're going to?"

"Yeah. My dad says they got everything. It's a college town. There's a big university there."

"That's not all bad," Monk said. "Maybe I'll come out and visit you and see a football game."

"Would you really?"

"Sure."

We shook hands on it, and funny as it sounds, that's when it really sunk in that I was leaving. When Monk and I shook hands on his promise to come visit me in Arborville.

And so with the help of a couple of funny movers named Mike and Tony we packed all our stuff. Then the movers in a big green-and-yellow van headed for the Mass. Pike while we took off for Michigan in a different direction. Dad had decided to make our trip a vacation. And so he took us to Michigan the long way. By way of Montreal and Quebec. We camped in provincial parks and went way north, almost to Hudson Bay. Then we worked our way south into Michigan.

"I just want to prove to you that there's land farther north than Michigan," Dad said.

We crossed from Canada into Michigan at a place called Sault Ste. Marie. We took a boat ride there and saw the Soo locks and then we drove down through the Upper Peninsula and over the biggest bridge I'd ever been over in my life. Maybe not longer than the Bay Bridge back in California, but it felt higher.

The water below us—Lake Michigan and Lake

Huron—was oh so blue, and there were lots of sail-boats. Peggy accused Dad of trying to sell us on the move by taking us the pretty way instead of the direct route, which would have taken us through cities like Buffalo and Detroit.

We knew from all our moves that that's what real estate agents did when they wanted to sell you a house. They took you to it through nice neighborhoods.

Dad just shook his head and said it was a sad state of affairs when a man couldn't take his family on a pretty drive without being accused of having an ulterior motive. I asked him what that word meant, and he said it was just another way of saying tricky.

"Be tricky," I said. "It's nice."

We camped at a state park south of the bridge. Peggy and I were getting really good at pitching the tent and blowing up the air mattresses and laying out the sleeping bags. Then Peggy and I would look for wood while Dad got out the Coleman stove, and before you know it we'd have a big fire going and Dad would have the dinner cooking and it was nice. Dad was a good cook. So was Peggy when she wanted to be.

Sitting around the fire afterward was always when I thought of Mom. She'd loved camping more than any of us. We'd camped all over California and Oregon when I was small. Mom knew about wildflowers and trees and birds. Dad went along like a good sport. But he wasn't the camping type. Mom was the explorer. She always found the nature trails or wanted to see around the next cove. It took at least two years after Mom died before Dad broke out the camping equipment and we did it on our own—the three of us. And it was hard.

A state park south of the bridge was the last place we camped in, because we were due in Arborville the next day around noon. Dad, being an engineer, had it all worked out. He wanted us to get there about an hour before the moving van did.

During our trip I thought about our two movers from Boston (they'd let me help put our bikes into the van at the end) and how they must be going to Michigan by way of Florida if we were all going to arrive at about the same time.

Anyway, that last night camping we sat around the fire. Dad drinking coffee and Peggy and I looking into the flames. No one said anything for a while, and finally Dad looked across the fire at us and said, "Well . . . we start a new chapter tomorrow."

I snorted. "And next year we'll start another one when we move to someplace like Alabama." Dad looked startled when I said that. But I wasn't really sore. Camping had been too much fun to feel sore about anything. I was just observing what I thought was a fact.

Dad smiled. "I don't think so, Robby. I think this really is it."

Peggy and I looked at him. The light from the fire was dancing in his glasses. Dad wore old-fashioned

9

wire-rimmed glasses. I remember once for school in Watertown we had to write a description of our parents. Mine was boring. I would have had an easier time describing Mom, because she looked so . . . so different. But Dad was hard to describe. He just doesn't look unusual. He has thinning, sandy hair, a round face, the glasses. He's quiet, you wouldn't pick him out of a crowd. He's very smart, but even that doesn't show. Now, as Peggy and I looked across the campfire at him, I think we both had the same thought: Something was going on inside his head that we didn't know about. Maybe there was more to this move from Massachusetts to Michigan than met the eye.

Peggy went fishing. "How do you *know* this move is it?" She tried to keep her tone casual. She fooled Dad, but she didn't fool me.

"Well, I think it's the kind of job and it's the kind of place and . . ." He didn't finish the sentence.

Dad usually finishes his sentences, but he didn't finish that one. He seemed embarrassed.

"How is this job different from your other jobs, Dad?" I asked, quickly.

I hate seeing Dad embarrassed. Also, the fact is, Peg and I hadn't really ever talked with him in detail about this new job in Arborville. I guess we thought it would be like all his other jobs. Dad always worked for software companies, creating programs for all kinds of businesses. The software companies always had names like Icarus or Daedalus or Photonics. Once I asked Dad to ask his boss at Photonics in Watertown if they would sponsor our baseball team, but they wouldn't. I guess high-tech names didn't go with baseball. We were always Acme Furniture or Lardas Dry Cleaners or Jack's Texaco.

"How is this job different from my other jobs?" Dad repeated my question. "Well, to start with, Robby, I'm going to be a part owner."

"Wow. You never told us that," we said.

"Well, I guess we didn't really want to talk about it, did we? Neither one of you was keen on leaving Massachusetts, and I was upset that you were upset. So we never really got around to talking about the new life I was going to lead."

"New life" was pretty deep stuff.

Peggy said, "Is being an *owner* all that different?" She wasn't satisfied yet that he'd told us everything.

"I think it will be a lot different, Peg. It will entail risks you don't have when you work for someone else. On the other hand, there are big rewards if your company does well."

It was odd to finally talk about why we were moving when we were almost there. Dad told us the whole story. Or at least, looking back on it, part of the whole story. A guy he knew from California had moved his family back to Michigan, where he came from originally. And in this town called Arborville he had started a software company. The problem was that it wasn't doing too well. Neither were he and his wife. They ended up getting divorced, and in the settlement she got the company. She didn't know anything

11

about running a computer software company—she was a real estate agent—and so she wrote to Dad and asked him if he would come out to Michigan and look at the business and tell her whether it was worth keeping and hiring someone to run it better than her ex-husband had, or should she just try to sell it. Dad went out to Michigan—I remember when he went we thought it was just another ordinary business trip. He went out there and looked at the books and contracts they had and the programs they were creating and he checked out the local markets, and he told her that even though the company had had a shaky start, it had potential and was worth keeping. And then, he said, he did something that surprised him, because he's not an impulsive person: He offered to buy it. Dad laughed. "Having told her it was worth keeping, I offered to buy it from her. To my surprise she made a counteroffer that, as they say, I couldn't refuse."

"What was her counteroffer?" Peg asked.

"To be a fifty-fifty partner with her. I'd run the company and share the profits, but I wouldn't have to put up any money to buy in—just get it going again. Offers like that don't come along often."

I remembered then that Dad had come back from that Michigan trip and had seemed different. Even quieter than he usually was. He didn't even talk about the trip. And we didn't ask, but Mrs. O'Rourke, our housekeeper, noticed it too, and said she was sure "your fathuh made a big killing in Michigan." That is how they say "father" in Boston. Mrs. O'Rourke lived just down the block from us. She was an older woman whose kids had grown up, and Dad paid her a hundred dollars a week to clean our house, to be there when we got home from school, and to cook the evening meal for the three of us.

Thinking about Mrs. O'Rourke, who had cried when we left, made me ask Dad if we were going to have a housekeeper in Michigan, too.

"Of course," Dad said. "Being an owner means, certainly at the beginning anyway, that I'll be working eighteen hours a day. I'll probably have to do a lot more traveling. If I'm to get the company going, our customers will have to be all over the country."

"Then it's too bad Mrs. O'Rourke couldn't come with us," Peggy said.

"And Monk Kelly too."

"You'll make friends, Robby—"

"Not like Monk."

"One of the things you learn as you get older, Robby, is that good people are everywhere. Like Monk. Like Mrs. O'Rourke. I'm sure we'll find a new Mrs. O'Rourke in Arborville, even though I'm also sure she'll be a different sort of person."

"What do you mean by that?" Peggy asked. Her voice was suspicious.

Dad either missed it or ignored it. "What I mean, Peg, is that you're both older moving to Arborville than when we moved to Watertown. I don't think we need to have someone there to meet you after school.

13

We won't need a housekeeper to put in all the hours Mrs. O'Rourke did." Dad paused. "Ruth has put an ad in the *Arborville News* for us looking for a graduate student at the university who'd be willing to exchange room and board for some light housekeeping and cooking the evening meal. I don't anticipate a problem replacing Mrs. O'Rourke."

He had slipped that "Ruth" in deftly, but neither Peggy nor I missed it. I didn't want to ask though. Peggy had no hesitation. "Who's Ruth?" she asked bluntly.

Dad didn't bat an eyelash. He'd been expecting the question. And probably wanted it. "Ruth is Ruth Lowenfeld, Art Lowenfeld's ex-wife. Art Lowenfeld was the person who started the company."

"You mean this Ruth is your new partner?"

"That's right, Peg."

Peggy was frowning. I didn't quite know what she was getting at, but it made me uneasy.

"Can I ask something?" I said.

Dad nodded.

"Room and board . . ." I said. "Doesn't that mean the housekeeper is going to live with us?"

"That's exactly what it means, Robby."

"I got news for you. I'm not sharing my room with a housekeeper."

Dad laughed. "Ruth has rented us a big house."

"Can we talk some more about this Ruth?" Peggy asked.

Dad took off his glasses and wiped them carefully.

He always did that when he was being extra cautious. "What do you want to know, Peg?"

"Why she asked *you* to come out to Michigan to look at this company?"

"That's a fair question. We only knew the Lowenfelds socially in California, and then not very well. You didn't know them, Peg, because they lived in Sunnyvale. I think the reason she asked me was because I *didn't* have a close business connection with her husband. In fact, we were really competitors, working on the same sort of software programming. Which is one reason we weren't close. Thus I suspect she felt she could trust me for an objective opinion."

"Did she know Mom?"

"We all knew each other casually." He smiled at Peggy. "I think you're going to be a district attorney when you grow up."

Peggy didn't smile the way he wanted her to. D.A.s don't smile. "If you don't get along with this Ruth Lowenfeld . . . if you have business disagreements and it doesn't work out . . . what happens then? Do we move back to Watertown?"

"Good question," I said.

"It's not a good question. It's an iffy question," Dad said. "That's a bridge you only want to cross if you come to it. Of *course* we could move back to Watertown. We could also move back to California. We could, as Robby cynically suggested a few minutes ago, even move to Alabama. Listen, I think we have some marshmallows to toast. Robby, would you get them out of the sack?"

"You guys got sticks?" I asked.

"I do," Dad said.

"I don't want any marshmallows," Peggy snapped.

"That's a first," I said. "I get yours."

"Since Mrs. Lowenfeld has rented a house for us and put an ad in the paper for us, does she also get to pick the housekeeper?"

Boy, I thought, Peggy would just not let up. Dad was patient, though.

"No, I think the three of us will pick the housekeeper."

"How many marshmallows do you want to start with?"

"Two," Dad said. "And give Peggy two."

"She doesn't want any. She doesn't even have a stick."

"She can use mine."

"I'll toast both sticks. What's the name of your company, Pop?"

"Computel."

"Sounds legit." I stuck two sticks and six marshmallows, three on a stick, out over the fire, not letting them touch the flames. "You think Computel might sponsor a kids' baseball team?"

"I don't see why not."

That was good enough for me. I shut up and concentrated on the marshmallows. You can ruin a good marshmallow by not concentrating, and burning it. Peggy was just getting rolling though. She went on asking questions. Not about Ruth, but about the house we were renting. Did it have a garden, and if so what was in it? Did it face north or south, and how far was it from our schools? Stuff Mom would have asked. It was almost like Peggy was sitting in for Mom. Which I guess in a way she was. Mom's death had been harder on Peg than me, I think. One night in California soon after Mom died, Dad caught Peg studying Mom's recipes. Peg was eleven. He made her put them away. "You don't have to be Mom, Peg," he said softly. She started to cry. Together they put the recipes back in order and the box away.

I wondered if that was starting again and why. Maybe it was the move. I didn't want to move again any more than she did, but, heck, here we were, almost there. And Dad deserved a shot at his own business. I wished Peggy would get off his back. But she didn't. Though I did notice she ate her marshmallows, and even had four more.

Cities are tough nuts to crack.

When we first went to Massachusetts, we saw it from the air, which means we didn't see it at all. From twenty thousand feet up it was a lot of toy houses and giant footprints that were sand traps in golf courses, and you couldn't tell what was Watertown or Boston or Malden or anything. As we looked down from the plane, all I thought was: We're going to have to live in that mess. But after you get on the ground and live there a while the mess turns out to be kids and backyards and short cuts and it all turns out okay.

Coming into Arborville by car was different. We came over the crest of a hill on the interstate, and there were big buildings. We were *below* this town, which didn't look like a town at all. It looked like a city.

"What's going on?" I said. "I thought Arborville was a small town."

"What made you think it was a small town?" Dad asked.

"It sounds like a small town. Arborville. That doesn't sound big."

Dad winked at Peggy but she didn't smile. Dad said, "Since when did towns start sounding big or small?"

"They just do."

"What towns sound big?"

"New York, Boston, San Francisco."

Dad laughed. I was one of the few people who could make him laugh. Though this time I didn't know what was so funny. Dad said he'd tell me a joke that would explain the humor of what I'd just said.

Peggy and I raised our eyebrows at each other. Dad's an engineer. Engineers never tell funny jokes.

But Dad started telling one anyway. "A city man took his city son out to the country. The son had never seen farm animals before. They went over to the pigpen, where there were some pigs rooting around in the garbage. 'Daddy, what are those?' the son asked. The father said, 'Son, those are pigs and rightly so called.' "

Dad laughed. He laughed alone. I didn't get it. And neither did Peggy.

"What's so funny?" Peggy asked.

"Oh," Dad said. "Well . . . if I have to explain it, it won't be funny."

"Better not explain it then," I said.

19

Dad laughed again. He was in a pretty good mood. Unlike me and Peg. He was excited about the move. We were apprehensive, which is another word for scared.

Soon we exited off the interstate where it said Downtown Arborville and were moving down a city street that seemed lined with junkyards on one side. There was a river there, but you couldn't see it for the junkyards. Not a great start to a new town.

"Do you know where we're going?" Peggy asked.

"I think so. This road should take us into Main Street, and according to Ruth, once we're on Main Street we can take just about any left toward the campus area. We don't live far from the university."

"Did *Ruth* also tell you to take us camping?" Peggy asked.

"Aw, lay off, Sis," I said. Dad isn't usually a happy guy, and I thought it was mean to ruin his mood. I gazed out the window. "This looks like Main Street anywhere. There's a dime store, a McDonald's, there's a video rental, drug store, restaurants, shoe store, department store. . . . Why do people move if everything is the same everywhere?"

Dad smiled at me in the rearview mirror. "That's not all bad, Robby. You might be a computer expert when you grow up. It certainly would simplify life if everyone stayed in the same place."

"Yeah, but then the moving van people would go broke."

Dad laughed. "I didn't think of that."

"I wonder if the van's there yet. Those two guys were funny. What were their names?"

"Mike and Tony," Peggy said. "They ought to be there. They were leaving right away."

"They had a partial load to deliver in Ohio. That was one of the reasons we could go camping," Dad said.

Dad wasn't sure which side street to take up to campus, so he picked one at random and we turned left, and sure enough in a few blocks we saw a lot of trees and college-type buildings and, best of all, the real giveaway: students. Although it was only the end of summer, there were already lots of college-age kids around. I started thinking: This may not be all bad.

Dad stopped the car and asked some students directions to Olivia Street, which was the name of our street, and naturally they didn't know. Everyone was from somewhere else. That's the rule when you're in a strange town. You can never ask directions from someone who lives there. Some towns you get the feeling no one lives there. Or maybe it's just that people who know where everything is stay home so they won't have to answer questions.

Finally we hit on a man with a briefcase who knew where Olivia Street was, and we got there in about two minutes.

In Watertown we'd lived in a small brick house. The house Dad stopped our car in front of was a large green monstrosity. Wood. Old. Three stories high. I couldn't believe it. I don't think Peggy could either. It was really ugly. Neither of us got out of the car. We just stared out the windows at it. Finally Dad said, "Well, here we are. Aren't you going to get out?"

"I don't think so," Peggy said.

"I know I'm not," I said. "That place looks like the house in *Psycho*."

"All right," Dad said. "You've had your jokes. Let's go."

"*Ruth* really picked out a beauty for us," Peggy said, not moving. "We're going to rattle around in there."

"Like skeletons," I added.

Dad didn't know how to manage us when we got this way. Mom would have spanked us both. Dad just looked unhappy.

"C'mon," I said to Peggy. "Let's go."

Peggy got out as though an invisible force was holding her back. She frowned at the house. "How many bedrooms are there?"

"I don't know," Dad said. "Four or five, I think."

"Didn't you ask *Ruth* how many bedrooms it had?"

Dad looked at her a moment before answering. "She told me, Peg," he said, trying to sound calm. "I don't remember now how many there are. Quite a few, I expect. The reason we have a big house is that I told Mrs. Lowenfeld we needed room for a housekeeper. That's why we have a big house."

Well, I thought, Peggy's accomplished one thing. He's off "Ruth" and back to "Mrs. Lowenfeld."

"It looks like we have enough rooms for an army of housekeepers," Peggy said.

"Peggy," Dad said patiently. "We're not *buying* this house. We're *renting* it for one year. Try to look at this as an adventure?"

"That's what Mom would have said," I said.

"Leave Mom out of it," Peggy snapped.

"But it *is* exactly what Mom would have said," Dad said. "She'd have said, let's give it a chance and see what it has to offer. Let's try to have some fun. Let's go exploring."

And with that, quoting Mom, Dad went up the walk toward the house. He was hoping, I knew, that we were following. We weren't. I gave Peggy a dig with my elbow. "How about cutting it out, huh?"

"You don't know what's going on, Robby."

"We're renting a house for a year. That's all."

"You dope. Don't you see what's going on with this Ruth Lowenfeld person?"

I stared at her. "What's going on?"

"She's getting her hooks into Dad. We're not just getting a new house, stupid, we're getting a new mother."

"You're crazy," I said. "You're absolutely out of your mind."

"Am I? Wait and see."

"Hey, you two, guess what I found inside."

"What?" I started up the walk. Peggy came too.

"A sign with a message on it."

"I bet I know what it says," Peggy muttered.

" 'Welcome to Arborville, Miller Family. Ruth Lowenfeld.' "

I hurried up the walk to see if Peg was right.

The sign, in crayon, said:

> **Welcome, Millers**
> **We expect you for dinner tonight. We'll be**
> **in touch.**
> **Ruth and Beth Lowenfeld**

"What did I tell you?" Peggy muttered.

"Who's Beth Lowenfeld?" I asked.

"Her daughter," Dad said. Peggy shot me a know-ing look. Dad knew the Lowenfeld set-up pretty well. So what? It didn't mean a thing . . . yet.

"Let's look around," Dad said cheerfully. "I haven't seen this house either. What do you think of the living room, Peg?"

Peggy looked at the living room as though it was a dungeon. It was just a big, old, empty room.

"Or maybe this should be the dining room and this room the living room. We can do anything we want. Isn't this going to be fun? What do you think, Peg?"

It could break your heart, Dad trying to make us happy about this move. But it wasn't going to work. Certainly not with old Peg. She could be stubborn. I wondered if she was right about this Ruth Lowenfeld. It was hard to believe. We didn't think Dad would ever remarry. Not after Mom. He'd never find another woman like Mom, who was so happy and smart and a sport for anything.

"I think this should be the dining room, don't you, Peg?"

In Massachusetts, Dad was invited to dinner parties a lot because a widower his age—thirty-seven— was a good catch. There's a lot more single women than men.

"And look at this kitchen, Peg. Look at all the space. Don't you think our round table will fit in here nicely?"

But Dad's a pretty cautious guy. And he's so wrapped up in his work. Peggy and I just never worried that he'd fall for some woman. Maybe it would be different with this Lowenfeld woman, but I didn't believe it. We came first with Dad. And then his work. Peggy was just getting into a lather about nothing, I decided.

"And this has to be the housekeeper's rooms. A bedroom and a little work room where she can study. And her own private bathroom. Don't you two want to see this?"

"Sure," I said. "If we're gonna help pick a housekeeper, we better see where she's going to live."

Peggy came too, and she unbended enough to admit it was nice. She wished *she* could have two rooms like that.

"Wait till you see what's upstairs," Dad said, and he bounded up the old wood stairs like an antelope. Though the truth is, I've never seen an antelope run up a staircase. Anyway, you had to love him for his enthusiasm and wanting us to share it.

"I wonder how old this house is," I said to Peg as we climbed up after him.

"I don't know. But she couldn't have picked out an uglier house for us. She had to do it on purpose!"

"Aw, come on, Peg. Why would she want to do that, if she likes Dad the way you say?"

"Did it ever occur to you that maybe she has a wonderful modern house that we might all be grateful to move into?"

"Boy, you've really got it on the brain, you know."

"Four bedrooms and a bath . . . a wonderful old-fashioned bathroom," Dad called out happily.

"That means it has no shower," Peggy said to me. "I hate taking baths. You lie in your own dirty water."

She was right about no shower. "We'll put one in right away," Dad said. "Well, shall we choose rooms?"

"Sure," I said. I ran from one room to another. They all looked alike. One, though, was clearly bigger than the others. That had to be Dad's room. That room and another faced onto the backyard. It was a big yard. Lots of grass to mow. But also lots of room to

27

have a catch in. We had almost nothing in Watertown.

The other two bedrooms faced onto the street. Between them there was a closed door.

"That leads to the attic," Dad said.

"I'll check it out," I said.

There was a light switch. I flicked it and went up the stairs. It was a huge attic. You could stand up in it. Stand up heck, you could throw a ball in it. It had a window on either end. This had to be the third floor of the house. What a great spot to have meetings. . . . This house may have looked ugly from the outside, but it had all sorts of nooks and crannies inside.

"I don't want any of these rooms for a bedroom," Peggy was saying when I came back down. "I'd like those two rooms downstairs."

"Peg, be reasonable. The housekeeper can't live up here."

Back home Peggy had a neat little white painted room with a white desk and a white bed and shelves for her books and her horse models. The rooms in this house were all dark brown wood and had an old feeling to them.

"Well, you asked me what I wanted."

"There's a great attic up there, Dad. Why don't we stick her up there? I think I'll take this room. I want the street side."

"That's my room." Peggy snapped.

Dad and I laughed. I chose the room next to hers

and Dad said he'd take the big room and use the room next to it for his computer.

"We'll get phones up here right away," he said. Computer people and telephones go together.

Just then we heard the blast of a horn outside. I looked out the window of my new room. There was our moving van. Big and green and yellow.

"It's them!" I yelled.

I ran down the steps. I was glad to see that moving van. It was a link with home. Maybe the last one. Also, it was a chance to test Arborville. Adults don't know this. Kids do. You can always test a new town with a moving van.

Two years ago when our moving van arrived in Watertown from California, a whole bunch of kids came around. They wanted to know who was moving in. Did they have kids? If so, what kinds? How old? Boys or girls? If boys, what kind? Athletes?

That was when I first met Monk Kelly. I can see it as clearly as though it happened yesterday. The movers from California had finished taking everything in the house. But the long metal ramp that led from the moving van over our front step and into the house was still up, and the front door was still wedged open. In Watertown, like in a lot of old cities in the east, the houses are all close together and close to the curb. So a ramp could go right into the house. Which this one did.

Anyway, those kids were asking me all sorts of questions, and this one kid whose name I didn't know yet all of a sudden lifted his bike onto the ramp and started walking it into the van.

"What're ya doin', Monk?" a kid yelled.

Monk didn't answer. He disappeared inside the van.

"What's he up to?" someone asked.

"Who knows?"

We found out right away what Monk was up to. He pedaled out of the van on his bike and shot down the ramp over our front step and right smack into our front hall where he hit the brakes and came to a skidding halt in front of my father. It was a great stunt. Everyone cheered, including me, and then everyone wanted to try it. When Dad recovered from his surprise, he calmly congratulated Monk and told the movers to remove the ramp. Later, Monk told me he liked doing stuff like that in order to "sign in with a new kid in town."

I was hoping our van would attract kids and someone like Monk might sign in like that, even though this house was a lot farther from the curb and the ramp wouldn't come close to reaching it. Still, you could do something with that ramp. But no kids came around at all.

Only the movers, Mike and Tony, with their Boston accents.

"How come you guys took so long to get here?" I kidded them.

"We went fishin' in Ohio," Tony said while Mike, who owned the truck, got Dad to sign the paperwork. After that they started to unload. I looked around. No kids in sight. Oh, there were plenty of college students walking by on their way to campus. They smiled at me and Peggy and kept on going.

I turned to Peggy, who looked as sad as I did. "I don't think there are any kids our age living around here."

"That's the least of it," she said.

Mike and Tony carried our living-room sofa down the ramp.

"What would you guys take to put that back in there and drive it back to Watertown?"

Mike said, "Don't like Abuhville, eh?"

"There's nothing to like here," I shouted after him.

"Peg," Dad called from the front hall, "would you help me tell them where to put everything?"

"He still wants me to like this house," Peggy said bitterly.

"The house is okay. It's the town that stinks."

"We've got to figure out a way to get back east, Robby," Peggy said.

It was kind of a funny switch. Because when Dad first proposed this move to Michigan, Peggy didn't really object. She had friends all right, but not really close ones. Not the way it was with Monk and me. Now she was wanting to get back in the worst way. But I knew it wasn't because of the house. It was because of this Ruth Lowenfeld woman, who we hadn't even met.

"Peg," Dad called again.

"Coming," she said, and went into the house.

Tony came down the ramp carrying two lamps.

"Can I get our bikes out?" I asked him.

In Watertown they had let me put our bikes in at the end, because Dad figured I might want to do some exploring right away.

"Be my guest," Tony said.

Mike wouldn't have let me, but I knew Tony would.

I went up the ramp and into the truck. Our bikes were tied together right by the door.

I untied Peggy's bike first and wheeled it down the ramp and parked it on the lawn. Mike came and got a small table. I waited till he went back inside the house. Then I went back into the truck and got my own bike. I was at the top of the ramp about to walk it down when a snazzy red Mercedes sports car pulled into our driveway and parked behind our station wagon.

Now what? Could the Mercedes be a welcome wagon? I didn't believe it for a second.

A smartly dressed woman got out of the Mercedes.

"You must be Robby," she said with a smile.

"Yes, ma'am."

"I'm Ruth Lowenfeld. And this is my daughter, Beth."

So this was the famous Ruth Lowenfeld. Well, she was different all right. I thought that if Dad had any ideas about her, he was stepping out of his class. She looked expensive. I mean, fashionable and hard driving. I took a look at the daughter. And it was almost a laugh.

The girl was chunky and had braces on her teeth. Definitely *not* pretty. She was also chewing a wad of bubble gum, which didn't help her looks.

"Beth, this is Robby Miller."

The girl snapped a bubble off.

"Beth, you can do better than that," Mrs. Lowenfeld snapped. Her voice was as sharp as Beth's gum snap.

Beth Lowenfeld shrugged. "Hi," she said.

"Hi," I replied.

"I believe you and Beth are the same age," Mrs. Lowenfeld said.

A lot of people in this world are the same age, I wanted to say, but didn't have the nerve. Why was I meeting her alone? Why wasn't Peggy here too?

"When did you all arrive, Robby?"

"About an hour ago."

"And how was your trip?"

She was polite, and asking all the right things. I hate it when adults are friendly and don't really mean it. Kids can always tell. The worst part is you think you've got to be friendly back. The whole thing makes you feel slimy.

"The trip was okay."

"We thought about your camping your way here from Massachusetts, didn't we, Beth?"

Beth didn't say anything. I *bet* she thought about us camping.

"Camping is something Beth and I haven't done much of. I'm not much of a camper. Neither is Beth's father. I think you're going to like living here, Robby. Arborville has a lot to offer a boy your age.

34

And you live near one of the best parks in town—
Sampson Park. The school you'll be going to is in
the park. You live very close to everything. Maybe,
Beth, you could take Robby over to the park and show
him around."

The woman was an arranger, all right. I started
getting nervous.

I also started to feel sorry for her daughter. Showing me around was probably just about the last thing
Beth Lowenfeld wanted to do. She'd probably been
playing horse models with her friends and had been
dragged off to meet us. Well, I was glad she didn't
want to show me around. The last thing a guy needs
is to be shown around a town by a girl. That's a
terrible way to sign in with guys my age.

Mike and Tony came out of the house just then. I
had to get off the ramp fast. And what faster way to
get off than shoot the ramp à la Monk Kelly and give
this girl something to think about. Which is what I
did. I shot down the ramp hitting the brakes halfway
to the house. Mike shook his head.

"Lad," he said with a little Irish accent, "we ain't
insured for high jinks like that."

Ruth Lowenfeld laughed coolly. "Beth, I think you
may have met your match. I'm going inside and see
how everyone is doing."

Which left me and Beth Lowenfeld facing each
other. Mike and Tony were inside the van.

"That wasn't such a terrific trick," she said. "I
could do that with no hands."

"So could I."

"Let's see you."

"Wait till they get out of the truck."

"You scared of them?"

"No, I'm not scared of them."

"Where's your sister?"

"Inside."

"How old's she?"

"Thirteen. You got brothers and sisters?"

"No."

"Just you and your mother?"

"And my father."

"Your father? My dad says your folks are divorced."

"They are. But my dad lives in Arborville."

"Oh."

"They're gonna get remarried."

"Really?"

"Yes, really."

Well, that was the first good news we'd had in a long time. Wait till I told Peggy. Would she ever be relieved. I was pretty relieved myself, after meeting Ruth.

"When do you think they'll remarry?"

"Pretty soon."

"Like how soon?"

"Soon. Did you want to leave Massachusetts?"

What did that have to do with her folks getting remarried? This was one strange girl.

"No, we didn't want to leave Watertown. It was a

great place to live. And this town is terrible. There are no kids my age around here. Back home whenever a moving van comes on the street a lot of kids come around. There's no kids around here."

She grinned. "There's kids, but they mostly live on the other side of the park."

"Where do you live?"

"On the other side of the park."

"Where's the park?"

"Down the block. That way. That's where the school is too."

Mike and Tony came down the ramp. Mike had our washing machine on a dolly. Tony had the dryer.

Tony winked at me as he went by. "Girlfriend already. Fast work, fella."

I felt my face turn red. "Thanks a lot," I said to his back.

"Smart aleck," I muttered.

"He talks funny," Beth Lowenfeld said.

"They're from Boston. Everyone talks funny there. I'd talk funny too, except I was born in California."

"So was I."

"I know. Our folks knew each other."

"Your mother died, didn't she?"

"Yeah. But we're all right. Me and Dad and Peggy. We do fine by ourselves. There's no reason for our dad to get married again."

I could tell what I was saying pleased her.

"You sure your folks are gonna remarry?"

"Positive."

"I gotta tell Peggy that. She has some cockeyed idea that your mom and my dad . . . you know. They're partners in business, you know."

"I know, and it gets me sore."

"What's it get you sore for?"

"It's my dad's company. He started it."

"He seems to have done a lousy job with it."

"That's what you think."

"Nope. It's what my dad thinks, and he knows."

"Well, he's wrong. And the movers are in the house. You gonna do it with no hands or just talk?"

If she was a guy I would've slugged her. I just might slug her anyway. "Okay," I said. "Then it's your turn." I walked my bike up the ramp.

"No hands," she called out again. What a snot. She was sore 'cause I called her on her dad's business. Fact is, if her dad had been a good businessman, her mom wouldn't have had to call on our dad for help and we'd still be in Watertown. And that was a fact!

I got on the bike. It was going to be harder than I thought. It's easy to ride no hands when you're moving fast, but you can't start out with no hands. You have to get started with hands. Which is what I did. I hit the pedal and steered and then halfway down the ramp I took my hands off the handlebars. I shot down the ramp and up the walk, concentrating hard, not looking up. It was the shout that made me look up.

Ruth Lowenfeld was standing in front of the steps, and I was heading right at her.

"Robby!" Dad yelled again.

I hit the brakes. Mrs. Lowenfeld jumped. She didn't have to. I wouldn't have come close to hitting her. In jumping, she hit her knee against the side of the steps and fell across them.

Dad was by her side in an instant.

"Ruth, are you all right?"

"I'm fine," she said. "Just a little startled." She gave a phony laugh. "I didn't know Robby was a circus performer."

"I didn't know it either," Dad said, embarrassed.

Peggy stood in the doorway, a half smile on her face. "Oh, he does worse things than that all the time, Mrs. Lowenfeld."

Dad looked at Peg amazed. "Stop talking nonsense." He turned to me. "I believe you owe Mrs. Lowenfeld an apology, Robby."

"I'm sorry."

"Apology accepted," Mrs. Lowenfeld said with a bright smile. "No harm, no foul, as they say in basketball. Well, I'm glad you all got here safe and sound. And how does six o'clock for dinner sound?"

"If you're still willing to feed us, it sounds wonderful," Dad said.

"Good, I'll collect Beth and do a few errands. I've got to check my calls at the office. When you sell real estate for Harry F. Burns, you're working eighteen hours a day. Beth?"

Beth was suddenly nowhere around.

"Beth!" Mrs. Lowenfeld called.

"She was here a second ago," I said.

"I'm coming," a voice said from inside the van.

And then down the ramp came Beth Lowenfeld on Peggy's bicycle. I couldn't believe it. And she was no hands almost from the top of the ramp. I don't know how she did it. She came down the ramp like a meteor and came shooting right at us.

This time we all jumped. It was Monk Kelly all over again! I had this girl figured all wrong. She was all right.

Signing in like that, Beth Lowenfeld did me a big favor. She took the heat off me. There was no way now Dad could scold me in front of the Lowenfelds.

As soon as he started walking them to their car, Peggy gestured for me to come inside the house.

"That girl's okay, Peg. She was no hands almost from the top. Do you know how hard that is to do?"

"I don't care how hard it is to do. Don't start liking that girl, because her mother comes with her. And we've got to protect Dad from that mother. What you did was just right."

"What'd I do?"

"You tried to hit her with the bike."

"I wasn't trying to do that, for pete's sake."

"Well, from now on you will. We've got to show that woman that when she takes on Dad she takes on two awful kids. Tonight when we go to their house for dinner, you and I are going to have the worst table manners ever. Elbows on the table, spill stuff, and—"

"You're nuts. First of all, Beth told me they're going to remarry."

"Dad and her? How does she know that already?"

"No, stupid, not our dad and her. Her father and mother are."

"Really?"

"That's what she said."

"I don't believe it. If they were going to remarry, why would she be partners with Dad in her husband's old business? And if they were going to remarry, wouldn't he be here with her welcoming us?"

"Not necessarily. He's probably got some other kind of job now, and he's at work."

"Maybe. But I think we better make sure. I just don't believe it."

"Robby!" Dad called. He was coming back to the house, a grim expression on his face.

"You better get out of here. I'll distract him. Go by the back door."

"Robby!"

Dad was coming up the front steps now.

I took off. Out the back door and around the house. As I got on my bike, I heard Dad ask Peggy where I was, and Peggy said she didn't know but didn't our round table look great in the kitchen?

That stopped Dad in his tracks.

"Do you think so?" he said. "Ah, Peg, I thought you'd come around to liking the house."

I pedaled away as fast as I could.

●

I saw a lot of green up the block. It had to be the famous park.

Biking toward it I noticed that ours wasn't the only monstrous house on the block. There were lots of big, ugly houses. And lots of people seemed to be living in them. In the front yards there were bicycles, motorcycles, mopeds, even a small old car or two parked on the lawns. If you could call them lawns. There was more brown than green. More dirt than grass. And it wasn't just 'cause it was August. It was obvious that no one took care of their yards. The hedges were all scraggly. Later I'd learn it was because almost every house on Olivia Street was a rooming house filled with college students who couldn't care less about front lawns or bushes or flowers. At the time I thought Arborville was just a lot uglier than Watertown.

Olivia Street ran into the park where the elementary school was. It was an old school. A big redbrick building with tall windows and a bell tower on top.

There was a parking lot on the side, and to the left of that a kiddies' playground. Swings, rings, monkey bars, a chinning bar, and a jungle gym. Beyond that and in front of the school there was a flagpole. Past the flagpole and off to the left was the rest of the park. It was a big park.

There was still another playground, a bigger one with swings and rings and monkey bars and a teeter-totter and a little merry-go-round thing. There was also a kiddies' wading pool with little kids wading in it. There were mothers there watching them like hawks.

Beyond the playground was where the park got serious. Ball diamonds—two of them. Two softball games going on with big kids. A basketball court with college-age kids going full court on it. There was a college-age touch football game going on in the middle between the diamonds. It was a serious touch football game, with substitutes and girls cheering, and they seemed to have set plays and everything. Past all that were four busy tennis courts, and people were sitting on the side of a little hill waiting their turn to play.

All in all, it looked like a great park if you were eighteen years old or more . . . or five years old or less. I didn't see any kids my age . . . unless . . . wait . . . there were some kids playing tackle football without equipment on a level piece of ground near the little hill. They could be my age. Bigger kids wouldn't play tackle football without pads. But kids my age would.

As I headed that way I saw they were playing three on offense and two on defense. One defensive guy did a pass rush, the other went out with the receiver. On the offense, one went out, one blocked, and one passed.

I watched a kid gather in a pass and the defender catch up with him and wrestle him to the ground. They weren't tackling very hard. And they didn't have any running plays . . . what with three against two. I wondered if they'd let me in. Then there could be running plays.

I biked up to what I thought were the sidelines and hopped off but didn't kick my kickstand down. I just stood there and hoped they'd notice me. Of course they did, but none of them said anything. Their game went on. I could understand it. I was like that myself when new kids showed up. Nobody likes a strange face. In Watertown I was lucky Monk Kelly signed in with me that first day because we became instant friends, and I became friends with his friends. It was going to be a lot tougher here in Arborville because the Monk Kelly here was a girl, even if she didn't act like one.

Finally there was a break in the football action. I took a deep breath and yelled, "Need another man?"

They looked at me as though I'd just spoken in a foreign language. Then one of the kids said, "You know where we could find one?"

The other kids laughed. I felt my face turn red.

I wanted to take off right then, but that would be giving them too much satisfaction, so I pretended I was interested in their game for a couple of minutes and then I sort of pretended I was late for something—I even looked at a watch I wasn't wearing in case any of them were watching—and then I got back on my bike. One of the kids trying to catch a pass fell down. He grabbed at his ankle.

45

"Oooh, oooh," he groaned.

"C'mon, Mort," one said. "Play over it, man."

"Play over it yourself, Littlefield. This hurts."

Another kid looked toward me. "You wanna play?"

"Sure," I said.

"Better give him a tryout, Joe."

"What's your name?" the kid called Joe asked. He looked to be the leader. Or maybe it was just 'cause he was holding the football.

"Robby Miller."

"Okay, Miller, go out for a short one. Button-hook right."

I ran out about fifteen feet, head-faked left and cut right. The kid shot a bullet at me. I caught it and pulled it into my chest and kept going. First impressions are everything.

"Hey, all right."

"NFL stuff."

"You're hired, man."

"Who's your agent, fella?"

"He don't have an agent. He's a walk-on."

They were cool kids all right. I couldn't tell if they were being funny or meant it. Or maybe it was both at the same time. They were richer kids than Watertown. Monk could eat these guys up alive.

Joe, the kid who had thrown the pass, took two steps to his right, cut left, and held up his hands. I fired a bullet back at him.

"Way to go."

"Winkelman, you've had it."

"You can't make the club if you're in the tub, Mort."

The kid with the bad ankle laughed. "I'm feeling better already."

They made me throw some more passes, and then I got in the game. I caught a long pass and batted down a couple and did all right. They were good ball players, but no better than Monk or any of the other kids back home. No one tackled hard. We played for a long time and then someone had to go, and that's always how games break up.

"See you, Littlefield. You going too, Kosmowski?"

"Yeah."

"Hey, remember you guys, we got a soccer game tomorrow."

"We'll be there," Littlefield said.

Those two guys left, and the rest of us sat around on the grass. I learned their names. Joe Dawkins, Tom Tomzik, who was a great blocker and the only one who looked like he could have been born in Watertown (he sort of looked poor), Mort Winkelman, who'd hurt his ankle and was kind of funny.

Joe Dawkins lay on his back with the football on his stomach. "Where're you from, Miller?" he asked, looking at the sky. A blue sky with wisps of clouds in it. It looked different than a Massachusetts sky. Higher somehow.

"Watertown, Massachusetts."

"Where's that?"

"Near Boston."

"You a Red Sox fan?"

"Yeah."

"Well this is Tiger country, man."

"You gonna live here now?" Tom Tomzik asked.

"Maybe . . ."

"What grade you in?" Joe asked.

"I'm goin' into fifth."

"So're we," Mort Winkelman said. "What school?"

"That one, I guess," I said, pointing to the old redbrick building at the end of the park.

They looked at each other. "We all go there," Joe said.

"Except for de Vito. He goes to St. Edmund's."

"He doesn't know de Vito," Tomzik said.

"Who's de Vito?" I asked.

"He's our pitcher," Joe explained. "Baseball season just ended."

"Badly," Mort said.

"Now soccer's starting," Joe said.

"Don't you guys have a football league?"

"No. Soccer's the big thing till you get into junior high." Tomzik looked at me. "You play soccer?"

"I guess I could if there was nothing else to play."

"You ever play soccer?" Littlefield asked.

"You mean like on a team? Organized?"

"Yeah."

"No. But it don't look so hard. You just run and kick a ball."

Joe laughed. "Yeah . . . that's it."

The others laughed too. I guess I'd said the wrong thing. I changed the subject.

"I played Little League baseball back home."

"What position?" Joe asked.

"Shortstop."

"That's locked up," Tomzik said.

"Is that where you play?" I asked.

"Nope. That's where the coach's kid plays."

"Is he any good?"

"It's a she," Tomzik said.

I spoke without thinking. "Is her name Beth Lowenfeld?" I asked.

They stared at me. "How did you know that?" Joe asked.

"I didn't know it. I just guessed."

So Mr. Lowenfeld coached baseball. That was a wrinkle all right.

"So how do you know her?" Joe asked.

I hesitated. Something told me to go careful here. "Her mom rented a house for us. She was with her mom at our house."

"That's right," Joe said. "Mrs. Lowenfeld's a real-estate agent."

"She works for the Harry F. Burns Agency," Winkelman said. "What'd you think of Beth?"

"She's a tomboy." I told them about Beth's great ramp stunt.

Winkelman said, "Beth would do something like that. She's got a lot of guts."

"Can she play ball?"

"She can field okay," Joe said, "but she can't hit."

"She wouldn't start if she wasn't the coach's kid," Tomzik said.

"She'd start in soccer," Winkelman said. "She's the coach's kid there, too."

"He coaches soccer, too?" That really amazed me.

"Yeah," said Joe. "He's better coaching soccer than baseball. He doesn't know anything about baseball, but he's okay with soccer."

"Coaching two sports, he's a real glutton for punishment," I said. "He must really like to coach."

"It ain't that," Joe said. "Tell him, Wink."

"Well, Beth told me—"

"Beth and Mort . . . " Tomzik said, and rolled his eyes.

"Cut it out, Tomzik. We live near each other. That's all."

"That's how those things start," Joe said, with a laugh.

"They're just jealous, Miller," Winkelman said. Everyone laughed then, including Mort. Then his face got serious. "Her folks are divorced. Mr. Lowenfeld's only supposed to have Beth two days a week and every other weekend. *But*, if he coaches her, right? He gets to see her four or five times a week and Mrs. Lowenfeld can't do nothing about it."

"That's why he volunteered to be our baseball coach even though he doesn't know anything about baseball," Joe said. "We tried to get him fired. We were two and eight this year, and we got enough talent to finish first. He can't coach. We even got our folks to talk to him, but he won't give it up, and on top of that the company he works for is sponsoring our team. And sponsoring costs money. So we're in a real fix."

"What's the name of your team?"

"Blockheads," Joe said.

"It's Block Electronics," Winkelman said, giving Joe a dirty look. "Things aren't that bad."

"They will be," Joe said. "The worst thing that could have happened to us was them getting divorced and his old company going busto."

"And him working for another one," Tomzik said.

"The old one didn't go all the way busto," I said. "My dad's taking it over."

"You're kidding."

"No. But there's something I don't get. Beth told me her folks were gonna remarry."

"Believe that and you believe in Santa Claus. Right, Wink?"

"Right. That's what she'd like to see happen, but it won't."

"Listen," said Joe, "we'd all like to see that happen because then he won't have to coach her all the time."

"You guys sure about all this?" I asked. This was really bad news.

Winkelman said, "I live next door to them, Miller.

51

My folks know Mrs. Lowenfeld pretty good. They ain't gonna remarry in a thousand years."

"What we really need is a new sponsor for baseball, and then we might be able to get a decent coach." Joe looked at me intently. "You said your dad owns Mr. Lowenfeld's old company. That Computel thing. How about him sponsoring us?"

I didn't know what to say. Just last night sitting around the campfire I'd asked Dad the same thing. But circumstances were different. Last night there wasn't any Mrs. Lowenfeld in the picture waiting to get her hooks into Dad. Now we had to protect Dad. We had to get him and us out of here . . . and back to Watertown.

Peggy was right. We had to make ourselves obnoxious to Mrs. Lowenfeld every chance we got. Starting tonight, when we went to dinner at her house.

Dinner at her house? I looked up. The sun was going down behind the school.

"I gotta go, you guys."

"Where're you livin', Miller?" Joe asked.

"On Olivia Street. A big green house." I got on my bike. "But I don't think we'll be there too long. See you later."

"What number on Olivia?" Joe shouted after me.

"I don't know," I shouted back.

As I took off I could hear Tom saying, "What's he mean they won't be there too long?"

"Heck, what's he mean he don't know his own house number?" Joe Dawkins said.

Any other time I would have laughed. But it wasn't funny now. I shouldn't have come over to the park in the first place. All I'd got was a lot of bad news. True, I'd met some kids my age and made friends, but there's no point making friends when you don't plan on sticking around.

7

The moving van was still in front of our house. Mike was carrying a box down the ramp.

"Your fathuh was lookin' all over for you, bustah."

Our station wagon was gone.

"Is my sister here?"

"She's gone too," Mike called over his shoulder. "They left you a note on the mailbox."

I laid my bike down and ran up to the mailbox. A note was attached to it with masking tape.

> Robby,
>   We looked all over for you. We've gone to
> Mrs. Lowenfeld's. Her address is 1445 Hermitage.
> Please meet us there. Go across the park.
> Take Granger Street to your left and keep going.
> It turns into Hermitage.
>   Dad

They were just simple words, one after another on the back of an envelope and written in Dad's tight little handwriting, but I could tell he was mad.

Well, there was nothing to do now but find Granger Street and then find Hermitage and Mrs. Lowenfeld's house.

"Excuse me," a voice behind me said, "could you tell me if this is eight-ten Olivia?"

I spun around. I hadn't heard anyone coming up. I was losing all my Watertown street smarts already. A lady was standing there, a newspaper in her hand. At the curb I saw a yellow VW.

"I don't know what the number here is. Wait a second . . . this is it. Yeah, it's eight-ten."

"Is anyone home?"

"I'm home."

"I mean, are the people who live here home?"

"I live here. The reason I don't know the address is 'cause we're still moving in."

"So I see. My name's Carol Gulden. I'm here about—"

"You mean like in the mustard?" I interrupted.

She sighed. "You must be in fourth grade."

"Going into fifth."

She nodded. "Definitely fourth grade humor. Well, I'm here about the ad in the newspaper."

"For the housekeeper?"

"That's right."

"You don't look like a housekeeper."

She laughed. "What does a housekeeper look like?"

When she laughed I saw she wasn't that old. I mean

she was probably in her twenties. She had sandy hair, blue eyes, freckles.

"A housekeeper looks like old Mrs. O'Rourke. She was our housekeeper back in Massachusetts, and she weighed over two hundred pounds."

"I see," Carol Gulden said with a straight face. "Well, the ad doesn't say anything about having to weigh two hundred pounds. It just says evening meals and light cleaning."

I laughed. She was all right. It was odd. But I suddenly had the feeling I'd known this person all my life. It wasn't a completely good feeling either.

"We didn't put the ad in," I said. "Some lady who's minding our business did. But to tell you the truth, I don't figure we're going to stay in Arborville very long. Maybe a month at the most."

Her face fell. "Oh. That's too bad. This sounded like the right sort of situation for me. Well, I probably ought to talk to your father anyway. Is he home now?"

"No."

"Do you know when he'll be back?"

I shook my head.

Tony carried two lamps into the house.

"If I left you my phone number, would you give it to him?"

"We don't have a phone yet. He couldn't call you."

She was silent a moment. "Well, maybe I'll come back later."

I shrugged. "That's up to you." I didn't see Mike coming out of the house. I went on, "But like I said,

56

you'd just be wasting your time. We're gonna be moving back to Watertown real soon." Mike laughed. "Pipe dream," he chortled. I could have killed him.

Carol Gulden looked at Mike's retreating back as he went up the ramp, and then she smiled and said, "I think I'll take a chance."

She fished in her pocketbook and came up with a pencil and paper. She wrote using the back of her pocketbook to lean against. "Mind you, this is only in case you get a telephone and decide to stay in Arborville. It's the number of a friend of mine with whom I'm staying. She can't let me stay on much longer. So if I don't hear from your dad soon I may be bold enough to come back in person." She handed me the piece of paper.

"See you later," she said cheerfully.

I didn't say anything. Why encourage her? She was nice, but there was no way she'd be our housekeeper unless, I thought, grinning, she was willing to move back to Watertown with us. I wadded the paper into a tiny ball and dropped it in my pocket. She honked her horn as she drove off. Jolly mustard woman.

Tony came out of the house. "So you're moving back to Watuhtown, are you, lad?" Smart-aleck Mike had told him.

He laughed all the way into the truck. He and Mike were a real pair of comics. They'd probably had a good laugh about me, but they didn't know anything about what was going on.

"Robby," Dad shouted.

Our station wagon pulled up in the driveway. Oh, boy. I ran to him on the double.

"Dad, I'm sorry. I lost track of the time."

"I guess you did." Dad got out of the car and started walking rapidly toward the house. I had to run to keep up with him. "Who was that person you were just talking to?" he asked.

So he'd seen that. I hesitated. "She was a college student looking for a friend. She had the wrong address." My first Michigan lie. But it was in a good cause.

Dad shook his head. "I was hoping it might be someone answering the ad." He looked up at Mike coming down the ramp with a chair. "How's it going?"

"I think we got a couple more hours' work. That should do it."

"We've got to go out for dinner, Mike. You'll probably be gone by the time I get back. We've done all our paperwork. Can I count on you to lock up? Pull the doors shut and make sure they're locked."

"No problem."

"Thanks. And thanks for getting here on time. You and Tony have a safe trip home now."

"We will. And good luck to all of you." Mike put the chair down, and he and Dad shook hands. Then Mike winked at me. "You'll get used to it, son." he said. "You got a nice house here."

I didn't answer.

"Okay, Robby. We're late. Let's move."

58

A minute later Dad and I were driving along Sampson Park.

"Where in God's name were you, Robby? We looked all over for you."

"In the park."

"Peggy and I looked there."

"Well, I was there. I met some kids and played football with them. Do you see that hill?"

"Yes."

"Well, just to the right of it there's a level piece of ground. You can't see it from here. That's where we were playing."

"Do you have any idea how long you've been gone?"

I shook my head.

"Over two hours," he said.

"I said I was sorry."

"Sorry's not good enough, Robby. You're not being very nice to Mrs. Lowenfeld. First that business with the bicycle. And now keeping us waiting. We've been sitting at the table wondering if you got lost somewhere. I told Ruth I'd take one last look for you back at the house. What is the matter with you, son? I thought I was going to have the hard time from Peggy, not you. It's you, of all people, who's been letting me down."

I felt lousy. We drove in silence. Finally, Dad said, "You can wash up at Mrs. Lowenfeld's house."

"Dad, I've got to tell you the truth. That person

59

you saw me talking to was applying for the house-keeper's job. Here's her name and phone number."

I purposely didn't look at his face. I dug the tiny ball of paper out of my pocket and unfolded it. The paper was so full of wrinkles it was hard to read. Dad's voice was small and tight. "Put it on the dashboard."

I did.

He didn't say anything for a moment. We were driving down a street with very tall trees.

"Sometimes I don't understand you at all, Robby."

I swallowed. "Sometimes I don't understand myself. I'm sorry."

He didn't say anything more. Neither did I. By that time we had stopped in front of an expensive modern house set way back on a beautiful lawn.

Peggy was right about a lot of things, including this, too. The Lowenfeld house was a lot nicer than ours. It wasn't going to be easy fighting this woman.

"Where was he, Warren?" she asked.

"At our house interviewing a possible house-keeper."

Dad was trying to make a joke out of it. Peggy looked at me curiously. She was sitting next to Beth Lowenfeld at the table. Beth was looking numb faced, as usual.

Mrs. Lowenfeld had changed her clothes and was wearing a yellow dress. She also had on long, dangling yellow earrings. I don't usually notice stuff like that, but all that yellow sort of hit you between the eyes. There were also yellow candlesticks on the table. And yellow flowers in a vase. Color-coordination city, all right. Mom hadn't been like that at all. There were also pale-yellowish wineglasses on the table. Too much.

"Is that right, Robby?" she asked. "Did someone answer the ad?"

"Yes, ma'am. And I'm sorry to be late."

Peggy flashed me a look of disgust. She didn't want me apologizing to this woman. She wanted me rude and badly brought up. But that kind of thing was hard to do . . . in front of Dad.

"Well, that's the best possible reason to be late. Was she a nice person? No, let's eat and you can tell us all about her later. Robby, would you sit there, please?"

"Ruth, I think Robby had better wash up first."

Mrs. Lowenfeld noticed my face and hands for the first time. She laughed. "It looks like you wrestled with the housekeeper. Beth, would you show Robby where the guest bathroom is?"

"It's down the hall," Beth said.

"Beth, I asked you to *show* him, please."

Beth Lowenfeld got up from the table. She had changed clothes too. She had been wearing Levis this afternoon. Now she was wearing a white dress. A tennis dress. It also looked like Mrs. Lowenfeld had made her brush her hair.

"C'mon," she grunted.

I followed Beth out of the dining area and into another area. It was a house of areas. A big house with one area flowing into another. The opposite of our old monstrosity, which was filled with small rooms.

"I met some friends of yours," I said as I followed her down the hall.

"Yeah? Who?"

62

"Joe Dawkins, Tom Tomzik, Mort Winkelman, and two other guys."

She didn't say anything.

"They seem like pretty good guys."

"Yeah? They think so too. Here's the bathroom. . . ."

"They told me about your baseball team and your soccer team, too. They said you had a lousy record in baseball. And it wasn't their fault."

For a second I thought she was going to punch me. Her lips curled in contempt. "Think you can find your way back?"

"Yeah," I said, and closed the bathroom door.

Well, I'd made an enemy there all right. Peggy would say good going . . . or would she? Probably Beth Lowenfeld didn't want her mother to marry our dad as much as we didn't want him to marry her. Maybe we ought to be friends and allies. I don't know. It's hard to be friends with a girl, I think. Well, better stop thinking and start washing up.

It was a pretty fancy bathroom. Two sinks. Real flowers. Tiny guest towels. And guess what color. God, we'd be in straitjackets if we had to live under the same roof with this woman. In our bathrooms we always left magazines and old newspapers on the floor to read. I messed up a tiny yellow guest towel.

When I got back they had started eating. "I hope you don't mind, Robby," Mrs. Lowenfeld said. "But we couldn't wait any longer."

63

"That's okay," I said grandly and rudely.

Dad shot me a look. But Mrs. Lowenfeld didn't seem bothered.

"So tell us about the housekeeper. What was she like?"

In between mouthfuls I told them about Carol Gulden. Mrs. Lowenfeld said she sounded nice. Peggy said she wouldn't be so nice after she lived with us for a while. We were really messy and never got anywhere on time.

Dad looked pained. Peggy didn't look at him.

"Like where were you before you started messing with the housekeeper?" she asked me, talking like someone in a B movie about high school.

I almost laughed. I didn't dare look at Dad or even Mrs. Lowenfeld. I told Peg about the park and those kids. It was like Peg and me were having a private conversation. It was wonderfully rude. Mrs. Lowenfeld interrupted us to say that the Winkelmans lived next door and they were a wonderful family. Mr. Winkelman was a law professor and Mrs. Winkelman was an artist. The Dawkinses, she said, were a big athletic family in Arborville. She didn't know anything about Tom Tomzik's family, if he even had one.

A real nice lady. I really began to feel sorry for Beth.

"I don't go to Beth's baseball or soccer matches. I do go to watch her play tennis."

I looked at Beth. She looked at me. I decided not

to let on that I knew *why* Mrs. Lowenfeld didn't usually go to Beth's baseball games and soccer matches. And did you notice her calling a baseball game a "match"?

"You said you'd come to our soccer match tomorrow," Beth said.

"I'll try to, dear."

Beth wanted her there. Made sense if she was still working on bringing her folks together.

"You play both soccer and baseball?" Dad asked. "And on boys' teams too! Beth, you must be an excellent athlete." Dad was making conversation. He didn't give two hoots about sports.

"Athletics is just about all my daughter cares for," Mrs. Lowenfeld said. She turned to Peggy, which was a big mistake. "And what's your favorite sport, my dear?"

"Chasing boys," Peggy said.

"Peggy!" Dad exclaimed.

"Oh, she chases them all right," I laughed, "but she can't catch them."

"I can too catch them," Peggy said with a straight face. "I just don't want to get pregnant . . . yet."

I thought Dad's eyes were going to pop out of his skull. Mrs. Lowenfeld's lips pursed thoughtfully. She looked at Peggy, and I think she knew exactly what Peg was up to. Dad, of course, didn't.

"Peggy, what on earth are you talking about?"

"Aw, Dad, you know what I'm talking about. At least three girls in seventh grade got pregnant last year. You know Eileen Brophy and Mary Fran Holdeman and . . ."

And on Peggy rattled. Making up one lie after another. Dad was flabbergasted. Beth Lowenfeld looked at Peggy wide-eyed. Only Mrs. Lowenfeld and I knew what was going on.

Dad finally put an end to it by telling Peg to be quiet.

"I think, Peggy," Mrs. Lowenfeld said dryly, "you'll probably find Michigan a bit more boring than Massachusetts."

She disappeared into the kitchen. Dad looked at Peggy as though he could kill her. But he couldn't talk, because Beth was sitting there silently, looking at the three of us. Peggy looked pretty pleased with herself. I had all I could do not to laugh.

Finally Mrs. Lowenfeld came out of the kitchen carrying a large platter of cut-up chicken. Mom would have served it whole. And had Dad carve it. And made a big funny deal of it. This was a lot more efficient, of course. Like having tiny yellow towels and no newspapers on the bathroom floor. The chicken, I hate to admit, tasted good.

"This is wonderful chicken," said Dad.

"Do you think it's better than mine, Dad?" Peggy asked.

I laughed. Dad just stared at Peggy, who went merrily on talking about all the different ways she could cook chicken and how she had all of Mom's great recipes and how Mom's food was the only kind Robby

and she would eat. It was kind of an amazing per-
formance.

But for some reason it didn't faze Mrs. Lowenfeld.
She smiled at Peggy and said mildly, "I wish Beth
would take the interest you do in cooking, Peggy.
Now who would like more peas, chicken, potatoes?"

"I would," said Dad. It was his way of rebuking
Peggy.

I ate my food because it was good. But Peggy left
most of hers, announcing that she hated eating. She
had to keep up her figure. She looked at chunky Beth
pointedly. Mrs. Lowenfeld's eyes narrowed. But she
smiled. Boy, was she a tough lady.

"Then you probably won't want dessert," Mrs.
Lowenfeld said. She went into the kitchen and brought
back a fantastic-looking chocolate mousse. Peggy had
a great sweet tooth, but she right away said she
wouldn't touch it, though she often made chocolate
mousse for us.

That was too much even for me. "C'mon, Peg, when
did you ever make chocolate mousse?"

Peggy looked at me as though I'd stabbed her in
the back. Which in a way I guess I had.

"I think you were away at hockey camp at the time.
Wasn't he, Dad?"

I think Dad was in a state of shock. And even if
he wasn't (which he had every right to be), he still
wouldn't remember anything Peggy set in front of
him in the way of food. Food was just fuel to Dad.
You put a plate of food down in front of him, and

he ate it without even looking at it. Mom always said that really good meals were wasted on Dad.

Finally the awful meal, which really tasted good, was over, and Mrs. Lowenfeld asked us if we'd like to see the rest of the house.

"No, thank you," Peggy said coldly. "I really don't care for modern houses."

"Peggy," Dad said, his voice raised in anger, "I want you to stop right now. Ruth, I apologize on behalf of my daughter."

"Please don't, Warren. What Peggy just said pleases me very much. I feel now that I did the right thing in renting that lovely old Victorian house for you. You must feel that way too, Peggy."

Mrs. Lowenfeld's eyes gleamed with triumph. Old Peg was caught in her own lie. All she could do now was shrug and say, "Yes, I do." Again, it was all I could do to keep from laughing.

"I bet Robby would like to see our house, Beth. We have a Ping-Pong table in the basement. Why don't you show him around, dear?"

"Do I have to?" Beth asked.

"I'm asking you to," Mrs. Lowenfeld said gently, but you could hear the steel in her voice. I really felt sorry for Beth Lowenfeld. I wondered what her father was like. I sort of didn't blame him for splitting with this woman. Beth got up. "What do you want to see?"

"The Ping-Pong table," I said, grinning.

"Are you any good?"

"No. Are you?"

"Yes."

"Beth, a little modesty, please," Mrs. Lowenfeld said with a laugh.

"Well, he asked me. Come on, the basement's down here."

"Do you play Ping-Pong, Peggy?" Mrs. Lowenfeld asked.

"No. I'll just sit here with you and Dad."

The battle lines were drawn. I hoped Dad wouldn't get shot as the two women went to war over him. It was pretty funny in a way. Mom would have thought it was funny. She probably also would have put her arms around Peg and hugged her and told her not to fight so much. But Mom wasn't here, and Peg was a born battler. I wondered how it would all come out. Usually I wouldn't bet against my sister in a battle, but with Mrs. Lowenfeld . . . I don't know. She was tough and quick. And she had a lot of years on old Peg.

The Lowenfeld basement was really neat. There was a Ping-Pong table, a TV and VCR, a table hockey game, a dart board, and all kinds of posters on the walls. These people had money all right. Back home in Watertown we had an old cracked-concrete basement with bugs and mice in it along with our washer and dryer. Dad was always going to have it finished, but we never got around to it.

"You don't have to play Ping-Pong if you don't want to," Beth said.

"I'll play with you," I said.

We played. I could tell right away she was good. We'd never had a table. I wasn't a rackets person anyway.

"You play a lot, don't you?" I asked her.

"Not anymore. I used to play with my dad when he lived here."

"Is he any good?"

"Yeah. He's real good."

"My dad's no good at sports."

"My dad is," she said.

It sort of stung me the way she came back with that.

"I guess your dad doesn't know so much about baseball though, does he?"

"Who says that?"

"The guys on the team."

"That's their opinion," she said, and slammed a ball so hard it hit me in the chest. "You want to talk or play?" she said.

"Play," I said.

I'd have been better off talking. She beat me twenty-one to six. She felt better after that. I didn't.

"I bet you take tennis lessons," I said.

"What's wrong with that? It doesn't have anything to do with Ping-Pong anyway."

"You know what we call kids who take lessons back East?"

She waited for the insult.

"Tennis worms. They're not athletes. They don't

70

play football or hockey or baseball. They get money poured into tennis lessons. Every time they hit the ball you can see about fifty bucks in the swing."

"I play baseball and soccer. And I'd play football, too, if they had a league here."

"It's a good thing they don't. You could get hurt."

"So could you."

"Okay, you're wonderful. But I don't see any trophies around."

"They're in my room."

"I bet."

She looked at me. "C'mon," she snapped. And took off.

I followed her up the stairs. Did she really have trophies? I couldn't believe it.

As we went down the hall to her room I could hear Peggy telling Mrs. Lowenfeld that I got into trouble a lot in school back home.

And Dad said, "That's just not true. Don't believe a word of what she says, Ruth. It's pure sibling rivalry."

Well, Dad was fighting back.

Beth looked at me. "Did you get into trouble in school?"

"Sometimes. What about you?"

"I punched Joe Dawkins in the nose once. The principal made my parents come up after school."

"Why'd you punch him?"

"He said my father was a jerk."

Maybe that was a warning.

"This is my room."

Right off I could see I owed her an apology. There were trophies all over her shelves. No dolls in this kid's room. No horse models. Just trophies. A soccer trophy and a whole bunch of tennis trophies. There was a lot of gold in her room.

"What'd you do? Buy out a garage sale?"

"I earned 'em, smart aleck."

I went over to the shelves and examined the tennis trophies. City champ, 8–9-year-old division. Runner-up, 10–11-year-old. City champ, 10–11-year-old division. And lots of smaller club trophies.

"You gonna be another Martina Navratilova?" I asked.

Her eyes narrowed. She thought I was being sarcastic. I wasn't. I was impressed. She was really beginning to remind me of Monk Kelly. Monk had hockey trophies all over his room.

"Who's this?" I asked.

Propped among the trophies was a photograph of a man. He had a nice face, a smiling face.

"That's my dad," she said, giving me a warning look.

"He doesn't look like a computer engineer."

"Well, he is."

"The guys on the team told me your folks aren't going to get remarried." I wasn't needling her. I was trying to figure out a way we could work together.

She took the picture out of my hand and put it back on the shelf.

"They don't know anything," she snapped.

The door opened. Dad and Mrs. Lowenfeld came into the room.

"What a nice room," Dad said. He looked around. "What a bunch of trophies and . . . there's your father, Beth. What a nice picture. How is Art doing, Ruth?" Dad asked, turning to Mrs. Lowenfeld.

"He's doing fine," Mrs. Lowenfeld said carefully. I noticed Beth looking intently at her mother, as if challenging her to say something bad about her father.

"I'll be looking forward to seeing him again," Dad said. "Beth, I'm very impressed with all these trophies. Robby's a good athlete, but he hasn't accumulated anything like that. I'm sure the two of you will be getting together for all sorts of sporting ventures."

Only Dad would use an expression like "sporting ventures." Spoken like a true nonathlete. But you had to like him for it. Though I didn't much like the part about me having few trophies. If I wanted to, I could have told the Lowenfelds that Watertown wasn't as rich a town as Arborville. That towns in the East didn't throw around trophies.

"Ruth, thank you for having us. It was a wonderful meal."

"You're more than welcome, Warren. Can I count on you and the children for dinner here Sunday night? I'd ask you for tomorrow and Saturday, but Harry and I are showing some new condominiums near the golf course all weekend, and I'd never be able to prepare proper meals. But what about Sunday?"

"Ruth, you mustn't think you have to feed us."

She laughed. "Oh, I don't, but until you're settled I insist on it. Beth does too."

Beth Lowenfeld looked as insistent as a potato.

"Well, that's kind of you, and as soon as we get this housekeeper business settled, we'll have you back."

"Sunday it is, then," she said, smiling, "and I'll get in touch with you about the time. Now you'll need some staples for breakfast tomorrow. Eggs, orange juice—"

"Ruth, we're not even close to that. We've got to unpack our dishes. No, we'll eat out tomorrow and then buy some food."

"There's a Kroger's near you on Stadium Boulevard. And if you need anything before that . . . or even after—"

"I'll call. I promise you."

"Good. I'll hold you to that promise, Warren. Well then, good night, Robby." She leaned over toward me. For a scary second I thought she was going to kiss me.

I drew back. "Good night, Mrs. Lowenfeld." I turned to Beth. I felt uncomfortable looking at Mrs. Lowenfeld. You know how it is when you don't like someone. You don't want to look at them. Like you think maybe they can read your mind. And if anyone could, it was this lady.

74

"Come over anytime, Robby," Mrs. Lowenfeld said, and before I could do anything about it, she kissed me. I forced myself not to wince. Beth Lowenfeld looked on stony faced.

Peggy was waiting at the car.

"Where's Dad?" she asked.

"Saying good-bye."

"You should've stayed with him."

"She kissed me. I ran."

"Did she really kiss you?"

"Would I make that up?"

"You see, I told you. She's not acting like someone who's going to remarry her ex-husband."

"Oh, I didn't get a chance to tell you. They're not gonna remarry. Those kids I met at the park today gave me the real scoop. That's what Beth *wants* to happen. This kid Mort Winkelman who lives next door, his folks know Mrs. Lowenfeld real well, he says it's bunk. It ain't gonna happen. I wonder which house Winkelman lives in. Boy, there are some big houses around here. Did you ever see so many big lawns in your life? I wonder if that's where Winkelman lives. There's a boy's bike outside. Can you imagine leaving your bike outside like that back home? It'd be ripped off before you knew it."

"You should've told me about their definitely not remarrying before we started eating."

"Why? What would you have done?"

"I would have behaved a lot worse. I'd have really been obnoxious."

"I thought you were pretty obnoxious the way you were. All you could've done worse was spill your soup on her pretty yellow tablecloth."

"She didn't serve soup."

"She knew better. Hey, Peg, the woman's not dumb. She got your message. So did Dad. Look, I don't want to stay in this town any more than you do and I don't want that woman as my mother any more than you do and I don't want Beth Lowenfeld as my sister any more than you do, but we're not going to get anywhere by acting like jerks. You know how Dad is. He thinks he's got to like this woman and maybe even marry her 'cause she's being nice to him, but I don't think he really loves her. I think he's kind of scared of her, if you want to know. But you start tearing her down, and all he'll do is get his back up. You know how stubborn he can get. Real engineer stubborn. No, if we want to protect him from her, we got to come up with a real plan."

"Such as what?"

"I don't know. You think and I'll think, and maybe we can get Beth Lowenfeld to think too, 'cause she doesn't want to be related to us any more than we want to be related to her."

That sort of stopped Peggy. She couldn't imagine anyone not wanting to be her sister.

"Maybe we ought to help her bring her folks together," I said.

"How do we do that?"

"I don't know. I do know it can't be done by pretending we're awful to live with."

"But we really are. At least I am."

"I agree. But she's gonna be thinking you're only pretending. She won't know you really are awful."

"You're real funny, you know that."

We heard Dad's voice float over the lawn.

"We'll talk in the morning. Good night, Ruth." And then he came down the walk . . . *whistling!*

Peggy and I looked at each other. That whistle was the kiss of death for us.

"We better come up with something fast," Peggy said.

"Yeah," I said as the whistling got louder.

While we didn't come up with anything fast, we at least had the sense not to talk about our fears as we drove away from Mrs. Lowenfeld's house. Dad drove home with a cheerful little smile on his face. It was scary. Peg and I hardly dared look at each other.

But we managed to exchange a few words up in my room while Dad was puttering around downstairs, getting a start on putting things away.

"Have you thought of anything?"

"No. Have you?"

She shook her head. "I'm too tired. But tomorrow, Robby, we've got to come up with something. Time is working against us."

"So's she."

"I hate her."

"So do I."

Peg looked at me and then smiled and gave me a hug. Which told me how worried she really was.

"We'll think of some way to wake up Dad. Get a

good night's sleep, little brother."

"Good night, Peg."

In the morning we went out for breakfast and then looked for the Kroger's she had told us about. It took some time to find it. We got lost more than once. After that, it took forever to buy food.

For one thing, Peggy made a production out of it. As though she really was going to do all the cooking from now on.

"We'll need Chinese noodles," she said at one point. "I intend to make California casserole this week-end."

California casserole was one of Mom's big dishes.

It was lost on Dad. He just smiled and said, "Sounds fine. Get some."

Peg also insisted on buying artichoke hearts, because Mom liked to have them around. Who knew what we would do with them. But we also got regular food and toilet paper and a broom and a dustpan and a mop and soap and dish rags and paper towels and Brillo and on and on.... The bill was over one hundred dollars.

After that we went back to the house and put away the food. For lunch Dad made us sandwiches, and we ate among the boxes. After lunch . . . it was un-packing time. And that went on and on and on.

Every once in a while Dad would straighten up and rub the small of his back. "You know, I ought to run over to the office for a bit. They don't expect me till Monday, but . . ."

We never said anything. He would see us looking tired, and smile and say, "They can wait till Monday."

We'd work more, another hour or two, and Dad would rub his back again. "I ought to run out and get some phones. We're really all set with the phone company. All I've got to do is plug in some phones. We ought to go out and buy some phones."

But he didn't run out and get some phones. We just kept pecking away at the boxes, making space in and around them, until finally about six o'clock Dad called a halt. "Rome wasn't built in a day, and we won't get unpacked in a day. Let's wash up and go to dinner. Ruth gave me the name of a good restaurant."

Peg and I went upstairs to wash up.

"*Ruth* is running our lives," Peggy muttered.

"Any ideas yet?" I asked her.

She shook her head.

"The worst part is, every time we unpack something and put it away, I think we'll never get out of this town."

"Getting out isn't as important as getting him away from *Ruth*," Peg said.

"It'd be nice if we could do both."

"Shh," she said.

We heard Dad's footsteps on the stairs.

We found Mrs. Lowenfeld's "good" restaurant near the university campus. You could tell right away it was a fancy place because, when the waitress asked us if we wanted drinks and Dad said, "No, I think we'd better order," she disappeared and returned fifteen minutes later with leather-bound menus the size of our world atlas, and then disappeared again.

"I hate slow food," I said.

"You can order anything you want," Dad said, looking over the menu. "The sky's the limit."

He had to feel guilty to say that.

"I wonder why she likes this restaurant," Peg said pointedly.

Dad kept reading the menu. "It has good food and it's nearby. Incidentally, Ruth tells me that Arborville has many fine places to eat. There are French, Italian, German, Indian, restaurants. There's even a Thai restaurant. How would you like to eat in a Thai restaurant tomorrow?"

"I thought I'd cook chicken tomorrow and make Mom's California casserole on Sunday," Peggy said casually, looking at the menu.

"We're going to the Lowenfelds' on Sunday, Peg," Dad said equally casually.

"We don't have to impose on her like that, Dad. I can cook." She turned a page in her menu. It had all the earmarks of a matter-of-fact, run-of-the-mill conversation.

"She made a great point of wanting us, Peg. I don't think it would be imposing at all." Dad turned another page. "We agreed to go."

It made me want to scream at them both, the way

they were fighting through the menus and the casual-seeming talk.

"We can change our minds, can't we?" Peg asked, in a bored way.

"I think it would be quite rude, Peg."

"I don't think it would be rude at all. People change their minds all the time."

I tried to warn Peg with a look that she was treading on dangerous ground. Maybe she'd forgot how rude and obnoxious she had been at Mrs. Lowenfeld's dinner last night. Dad hadn't brought it up once, but that didn't mean he didn't remember. Dad liked to keep things in little compartments, and he'd most likely put it away in temporary storage. Leave it there, Peg, I thought. Quit while you're ahead.

"If you don't want to, I'd be happy to call her and tell her we can't come," she said, and flipped some more pages.

"No," Dad said. "We're going there Sunday night. Hmm, those lamb chops look good."

Peg closed the menu book. "I don't want to go back there, Dad," she said bluntly.

Go easy, Peg, I thought.

"Oh? Why not?"

Peggy went easy. Like a bulldozer.

"Because I don't like her."

Dad didn't get mad. He closed his book calmly.

"You don't even know her."

"I know her well enough to know I'm never going to like her. And neither is Robby."

Thanks, Sis, I thought.

Dad looked at me. There was a plea in his eyes. I felt so sorry for him. I sort of hated throwing cold water on him.

"She's all right, I guess." Peggy shot me a reproachful look. "But she's not like Mom," I added quickly.

"No," Dad said. "She's not like Mom. But I'm never going to meet another woman like Mom."

"You don't know that," I said.

"I think you're giving up pretty fast," Peggy said. "There's lots of nicer women than her around."

"She's a very nice lady, Peg," Dad said quietly. He was hurt. I wished Peggy would shut up. I wished we would all shut up.

"Ruth Lowenfeld is a bright and sensitive person. She's been through some bad times, and now she— "

"Wants a new husband," Peggy interrupted.

Dad was startled. And then angry. He controlled himself. "That's not what I was going to say. I was going to say, and now she is making a new life for herself. As for the new husband part, I really hate to hear you talk like that, Peggy. You're smarter than that, and nicer too. You don't have to talk that way. Nor, since you brought up last night, did you have to say the outrageous things you said during her very nice dinner."

Well, I thought, you did it to yourself, Peg. You brought him back to last night and to stuff he'd filed away. Congratulations.

"Chasing boys, pregnant girls . . ." Dad shook his head. "It was embarrassing to me. Fortunately, Ruth is an understanding person. She understood why you said all those things. She knows what we're all going through."

"And just what are we all *going through*?" Peggy asked, sarcastically.

"Change," Dad said. His face was serious. "Our world changed when your mother died, and we worked hard to make a new life for the three of us. Now that new life is changing again. Change is always frightening, Peggy. For everyone, including me."

"Can I say something?" I said.

"Please do."

"We're happy. We're okay. Why do our lives have to change at all?"

"Lives change whether you want them to or not, Robby. Life means change. In your case change is growing up. In my case change is growing old."

"You're not that old." I wished the waitress would come and rescue us from ourselves.

"I'm not getting any younger, son."

"Neither am I," Peggy said cleverly. "Which means I can take care of us."

That was impressive, I thought.

Dad smiled. "Peg, you're all of thirteen years old. You can't take care of us."

"Better than *she* can."

It was head-to-head combat. And it made me very unhappy.

"Can we order? I'm hungry."

"Do you know what you want?"

"A hamburger."

"Robby, this isn't a McDonald's. It's a good restaurant."

"I'll have a good hamburger then." I was really just trying to loosen things up. But it didn't work.

"I think those lamb chops look good. But you can order what you want. I'll try to catch our waitress's eye. Do you know what you want, Peg?"

"Yes."

Just from how she said yes, I knew Peg wouldn't be ordering from the menu.

"What?" Dad asked.

"I want things to stay the way they have been. The three of us and only the three of us."

Her voice almost broke.

"How come waitresses never look at you in fancy restaurants?" I said.

They ignored me.

"All I can say, Peg, is that I hope in time you will learn to like, appreciate, and perhaps even love Ruth Lowenfeld."

Peg's face froze.

Come on, waitress, I prayed. Turn around.

"Does that mean you're going to ask her to marry you?" Peg asked in a tiny, muffled voice.

Why did she have to ask that? No good could come from putting Dad on the spot like that.

No good did.

"Yes, Peg, I believe I will be asking Ruth Lowenfeld for her hand in marriage." He said it formally. Like a wedding announcement.

I felt sick. I could have killed Peggy.

"But why? Why?" Peggy's voice rose. People turned around to stare at us.

Dad cleared this throat. "You need a—"

"A mother?" Peggy cried. "We have a mother. She's dead. That's all."

She was starting to cry. Tears were rolling down her cheeks. Everyone but our waitress was now looking at us.

"Don't marry her for our sake, Dad," Peggy cried. "We don't need her. I can do things."

And then she put her head down and sobbed into her hands. She covered her face, and her whole body shook.

Dad, pale, reached toward her. Toward her hands. I think he was almost crying a little too.

"Peg, I'm not marrying anyone only for your sake and Robby's. . . . I'm . . . I'm . . . lonely, Peg. I love you two very much. I have my work, and I love that, but . . . "

The pain coming out of his face was so awful I couldn't stand it.

I stood up and yelled, "Waitress!"

Finally, she looked our way.

And came running over.

"Are you ready to order?" she asked in a frightened voice.

"Yes," Dad said. He blew his nose. He cleared his throat. He turned to Peg. She shook her head. She couldn't talk.

"We'll get back to her. Robby?"

"I'll have . . . lamb chops."

"Sorry, we just ran out of the lamb chops."

So there was some good after all in not being able to get her attention.

"I'll have the hamburger."

"How do you want that cooked?"

"Any old way."

"I'll have the sweetbreads," Dad said quietly.

Sweetbreads were what Mom always ordered when we went out to dinner. They were supposed to be a delicacy. Something you never had at home. Peggy and I tried them once and hated them. They were awful. Animal innards, like liver or kidneys.

"Peg?" Dad asked, looking at her.

Peggy blew her nose. She took a deep breath. She looked up at the waitress. "I'll have sweetbreads too," she said.

She was back.

Well, it was a rotten meal. The hamburger wasn't as good as McDonald's, Peggy couldn't finish the sweetbreads, and Dad's mind was elsewhere. But at least we didn't fight anymore.

"Thanks for dinner, Dad," I said as we walked to the car.

"Yes, thanks, Dad," Peggy said quietly.

"You're welcome," Dad said. "You know, I don't think we ought to do any more unpacking tonight. What do you say to a short tour of Computel Company? It's practically on our way home."

You could read Dad easily. He was trying to put a happy cap on a bad evening. It wouldn't work, of course.

Neither of us said anything.

"Come on, you two. Don't you at least want to see why you were dragged out of Massachusetts? Don't you want to see our company?"

There was no mistaking the pride in his voice.

"Sure," I said, knowing he'd rather Peggy said it. But Peg wasn't talking. She wasn't being mean or anything. She was such a fighter, and she had given her all in the restaurant.

Ten minutes later we were parked in front of a small, three-story building.

"This is it?" I asked, astonished.

I was used to the sleek, low-slung, white modern engineering labs that lined Route 128 back home.

"Not the whole building," Dad confessed cheerfully. "We're just the third floor."

Peg and I looked at each other. For the third floor of a small, dumb, redbrick building she and I had been dragged halfway across the United States.

"Come on," Dad said.

He got out of the car with that old energy of his and bounded toward the building.

"He's going to ask her real soon," Peggy said

mournfully. "I can tell."

"Well, you didn't help matters by putting him on the spot like that."

"I wanted to clear the air."

"You did a great job."

"She can't be our mother, Robby. It won't work."

"I know that."

"We've got to do something fast."

"Listen, you two," Dad called from the front door, which he had opened, "the grand tour of Computel begins in exactly fifteen seconds."

I didn't want a tour of Computel, and neither did Peggy. But we went in.

It turned out to be the smartest thing we could have done. For me, anyway, it put a hopeful cap on a bad evening. For it was inside Computel that I began to see how we could get Mrs. Lowenfeld out of our lives and us out of Michigan.

Computel turned out to be a series of offices. There was one big room—Dad called it the main computer room. There were a lot of PCs around, and six or seven printers. A big chart on an easel that Dad called a one-line diagram. And there were shelves filled with manuals.

Dad said there were twelve people working for Computel. Eight engineer-programmers, including himself, two salespersons, an accountant, and a receptionist. Every programmer had a PC in the big room and one in an office too. They could all access each other as well as a big mini-computer.

There was also a conference room, a kitchen, a storage room, a library with magazines like *Scientific American*, *Computer*, *Byte*, *Electronic Design*, *Software Engineering*. They were all familiar, since Dad often brought them home.

There were tapes and diskettes all over the place, and wads of printout. The library had hardcover books in it as well as manuals. Stuff like *Handbook of Math-*

ematical Functions. Proceedings of IEEE. The kind of stuff Dad read on camp outs.

"And this is my office," he said proudly.

It was a handsome office. Big desk and a thick carpet, built-in bookshelves, and a computer, of course, and a printer.

"We're going to create a lot of exciting things here," Dad said. "Before he left the company, Mr. Lowenfeld hired some very bright young mathematicians who are working on a medical program for the Burn Center . . . how to manage their data. All that's good. But we're also going to work on business programs for doctors, and for other professionals as well. We'll create programs for all sorts of small businesses. Accounting practices, inventory systems, tax records. We'll be working on a program for fund-raisers, a church, a newspaper, and a public health clinic. One of our bright young mathematicians is creating software for robotic vision systems."

I loved seeing Dad's eyes alive and gleaming like that. "What's a robotic vision system?" I asked, feeding his fire.

Dad jumped out of his chair. "Come with me!"

He led us back to the main computer room. There he showed us a printout that made no sense to me. But he explained it clearly. Robots have to see what they're doing. They see with the aid of TV cameras that are programmed to make the links between vision and action.

"What do the robots do after they see okay?" I

91

asked. I liked computer stuff, and Dad had showed me how to use his PC when I was in second grade. He believed all kids should be able to work with computers as easily as they ran or skipped down the street. He's right.

"Fair question: What do the robots do after they see? In this case"—Dad picked up a wad of print-out—"we're programming for a manufacturing company in Toledo. They make robots for General Motors that paint cars, tighten bolts, stuff like that."

"You work for a company that works for another company?"

"That's right, Robby."

"Can we go home?" Peggy asked.

"One second," I said. "Can you sell that program to another robot manufacturer?"

Dad was delighted with my interest. "Oh no, son. That's a proprietary document. Copyrighted by us. The manufacturer owns the program. They wouldn't want a competing manufacturer to get hold of it. They're in competition with other robotics companies, just as we're in competition with other software programmers."

"Who's *your* competition?"

"Everyone, including the Japanese and West Germans." Dad laughed. "Locally, though, here in Arborville there's only Block Electronics."

"The company Mr. Lowenfeld works for?"

Dad looked surprised. "How did you know that, Robby?"

Peggy looked bored. That's how dumb she was.

"He's the coach, and they're the sponsor of the baseball team Beth Lowenfeld plays on. The kids I met in the park told me that."

"Well," Dad said with a quiet laugh, "it's a small world. Art Lowenfeld is the chief executive officer of a rival company. We were friends and rivals in California, and I don't believe there's any reason to doubt we'll be anything but that here."

"Why did the Lowenfelds get divorced, Dad?" Peggy asked. She was with us again.

"Peg, we're on a tour of Computel. This doesn't have anything to do with that."

"I disagree," Peggy said. "Mrs. Lowenfeld wouldn't have asked you to be a partner if she hadn't been divorced."

She had him there.

Dad sighed. "All right, Peg. The fact is I don't know why the Lowenfelds got divorced."

"Don't you think it's important to find out?"

"I'm sure I will someday."

It was pretty unscientific of Dad not to investigate something like that. If getting married again was a programming problem he had to solve, he would have asked all kinds of questions; but Dad, like a lot of engineers and scientists, was a very private person, and he respected privacy in others. I didn't, thank God. And neither did Peggy. We had Mom to thank for that.

"Can I ask a question?" I asked.

Dad was relieved. "Of course, Robby."

"Does Block Electronics work on the same stuff you do?"

"I'm sure there are overlaps. They're a software company too. Problems and solutions in high technology have ways of flowing into each other. I know that Art—Mr. Lowenfeld—was working on some of these same programs in California. Which indeed was one of the reasons Ruth asked me to appraise the business for her. For example, a project I started on in California and played with on my own time in Massachusetts is one I'll be working on here between business trips."

Dad went over to a work station and picked up some printout.

"This has to do with the general field of artificial intelligence. Specifically, I'm trying to create programs that will help physicians diagnose illnesses. The time isn't far off when we'll be able to program computers to analyze medical data and draw conclusions from it just the way the human brain does."

"Robot doctors?"

Dad smiled. "Not quite. Or, maybe, not yet."

"Who can afford that kind of programming, Dad?"

"Big medical research centers."

"Are there other people working on it?"

Dad picked up another wad of printout. "Oh, yes. Especially in cities like this that have two big competing medical centers."

Dad put the printout in a drawer. As though it had

suddenly occurred to him that it shouldn't be left out in the open. Well, I thought, where there was printout, there had to be a disk. And a backup disk too.

"What's the name of your robot doctor program?"

Dad laughed at how I wouldn't give up the idea of robot doctors. "Right now its file name is REX-COMP."

"Why REX?"

"It's a way of saying Rx, or prescription."

"Are you connected from our house here?" I asked.

"As soon as I get a phone I am."

Which meant there had to be a disk copy of REX-COMP in our house. Dad would be working on it at home as much as he would be here. Probably more.

All good things happen unconsciously. As in sports, when you're flowing without thinking. I wasn't asking all those questions because I had a specific plan in mind. I didn't, but almost out of nowhere one was forming in my head.

It wasn't a nice plan. It was kind of desperate. It would break rules; it would break laws. But I had no choice. I couldn't have Mrs. Lowenfeld as my mother.

Voices woke me. One was Dad's. The other's was . . . ?
It was familiar. I opened my eyes. Daylight flooded
the room. I jumped out of bed and leaped over two
unopened boxes and my baseball bat, and tiptoed
onto the landing.

The voices came from the kitchen.

Carol Gulden was saying, "I could start whenever
you want, Mr. Miller."

The mustard woman. I had forgot all about her.
She sure didn't waste any time.

"How about today?" Dad asked. He didn't waste
any time either.

"I could be here by eleven."

"Great. We could all have lunch together, and you
could get to know the kids and vice versa."

"I've met Robby, of course. And I want to meet
Peggy. But don't you want to see a resume or references? I mean, I've literally just walked in off the
street. And the fact is I have been a teacher and have

done child care before."

"Oh, yes, of course, references. Yes, can I see them?"

Dad sure was a great housekeeper hirer. I tiptoed over to Peggy's room and opened the door. She was asleep. I touched her shoulder.

"Wake up, Sleeping Beauty. Our new housekeeper is here."

"Go away, pest," she said.

"Okay, but just remember, you were supposed to have a say in hiring her, and she's being hired right now under your sleeping nose."

"Is this a joke?"

"No."

Peggy rolled out of bed. "I'll beat the daylights out of you if this is a joke."

Pulling a bathrobe around her, Peg went out to the landing.

"Do you have a car, Miss Gulden?" Dad's voice floated up.

"I've got a VW. And I guess you'd better call me Carol, Mr. Miller."

"Will you be able to move your stuff in a VW . . . Carol?"

The mustard woman laughed. "Easily, alas."

Dad laughed too. He liked her. I could tell that. And so could Peggy.

"Because if you couldn't, you could use our station wagon, and Robby and I could help you."

"Heard enough?" I asked Peg.

She didn't answer. She marched down the stairs.

I followed her. Dad had made coffee for Carol Gulden and himself. She was sitting at our old round table. Dad had what must have been letters of reference in front of him. Carol Gulden wore a gray sweatshirt with the words Green School Gryphons printed across it in green letters. On the floor next to her chair was a blue-and-yellow book bag filled with books.

They both stopped talking as Peggy stomped into the kitchen.

"May I ask what's going on?" Peggy demanded.

Carol Gulden looked at Peggy with a friendly smile. It occurred to me that sitting there like that, Carol looked like a jar of Gulden's mustard at that. There was her yellowish, sandy hair. She also had some freckles. Spicy mustard.

"Peggy, this is Carol Gulden, who's interested in helping us out with housekeeping and cooking. Miss Gulden—excuse me, I mean Carol—this is my daughter, Peggy." Dad looked uneasy.

"Hi," Carol said. She craned her neck to see around Peggy. "Hello, Robby."

"Hi," I said.

Peggy didn't greet her. She didn't even look at her. "I thought we were all going to interview the housekeeper," she said to Dad.

Peggy could be rude all right. What she started two nights ago with Ruth Lowenfeld she was picking up today with Carol Mustard.

"We are," Dad said, flustered. "We were waiting for you and Robby to come down."

"Is that why you offered to drive her stuff over in our station wagon?"

It was clear Dad had forgot his promise. Adults do that all the time, but only someone like Peg would hold them to it.

"All right, Peg, sit down and interview Carol."

Dad agreed too quickly for Peg. She was surprised. She froze. For the first time that I could remember, old Peg didn't know what to say.

"I guess I can ask questions too, can't I, Dad?" I said.

"Of course."

"Okay, then," I said to Carol Mustard. "What sports do you play?"

"What a dumb question," Peggy said, recovering her tongue.

"All sports," Carol said, with a smile. "I played on my college softball team."

"What position?"

Peggy groaned.

"Pitcher," Carol said.

"Slow pitch or fast?"

"Really!" Peggy exclaimed.

"Fast. It was the varsity team."

"Robby," Dad said, "I agree with Peggy's sentiments. I think you could put more germane questions to Miss—to Carol."

"What's germane mean?" I asked. And looked at her. "Do you know?"

"Robby, that's downright rude," Dad said.

My question didn't seem to bother Carol though. She smiled. "It means relevant. Pertinent. For example, more appropriate questions for someone who's going to clean your house and prepare some meals might be: Can you cook, can you clean?"

"Can you?"

Dad winced.

"Yes," she said.

"I vote to hire her," I said. "We've never had a housekeeper who could cook, clean, and fast pitch."

Carol laughed merrily. Dad, smiling, shook his head as though it was all too much for him. He turned to Peggy. "Peg?"

Peg launched an attack. "Why do you want to be our housekeeper?"

"I need room and board while I'm going to school."

"How old are you?"

"Peggy, I have that information right here on Miss— I mean—Carol's resume," Dad said.

"I'm twenty-eight," Carol said to Peggy.

"Isn't that pretty old to be still going to college?"

"Good Lord," Dad said.

"I think that's a perfectly appropriate question, Mr. Miller. It is old, Peggy. I've been teaching school in West Bloomfield for the past six years. I resigned last winter. I wasn't sure after six years of teaching that that was how I wanted to spend the rest of my life."

"What grade did you teach?" I asked.

"Fourth grade."

"So that's how you know about fourth grade humor."

"Right." She turned to Peggy again. "I decided a good place to come to while I was deciding what I wanted to be when I grow up was Arborville. Take some courses at the university. And earn a little money to pay for my room and board . . . not to mention tuition."

"Where are you from?" Peggy asked.

"West Bloomfield. Not far from where I taught."

Dad didn't stop us. He was interested in spite of himself.

"Where's West Bloomfield?" I asked.

"Outside of Detroit."

"What's your religion?" Peggy asked.

That stopped Carol. It also stopped Dad. He looked embarrassed. "I think there's been enough interview, kids."

"I don't mind answering that, Mr. Miller." Carol said. She turned to Peggy. "My father is Jewish, my mother is Protestant."

"What are you?" I asked.

"For God's sake, Robby. Not you too." Dad's face was red as a beet.

"I guess I'm a bit of both, Robby. I'm not religious, if that's what you're asking."

"We aren't either. Mom used to take us to church, but we haven't gone once since she died. Not even at Christmas or Easter."

I thought Dad would die.

"We could go if we wanted to," Peggy said.

"We just don't want to," I said. "I think if God was so hot he wouldn't have taken Mom from us."

Carol looked at me. So did Dad. For a moment no one said anything, and then Peggy said, "I have just two more questions."

"I do apologize for this," Dad said to Carol.

She smiled. "Don't. The openness is kind of wonderful. And it obviously cuts both ways."

"Doesn't it," Dad said.

I didn't get that. Later Peggy told me that meant Carol was learning as much about us as we were about her. I didn't see that then, though. What I could see then was that Peggy liked Carol Gulden. She wouldn't be asking all those tough questions if she didn't like her. I sensed that Carol understood that.

"Are you married?" Peggy asked her.

"No."

"Were you ever?"

"No."

"Okay," Peggy said with a smile. "I'm done."

"The prosecution rests," Dad said. "Well, that about winds it up. Now should we—"

"I'm not done," I said. They looked at me astonished.

"You ever coach a baseball team?"

Peggy snorted.

Dad said, "Well, we needed a little comic relief. And Robby has provided it. Now, do we ask Carol to leave the room while we take our vote?"

"No, Robby, I never have," Carol Gulden answered me. She took me seriously. I liked that. I really liked her. She was different from Mom but nice. Really nice. Why wouldn't Dad fall in love with someone like her instead of someone like Mrs. Lowenfeld?

"I taught phys ed my first full year of teaching. So I could probably coach baseball."

"I don't think we have to go out of the room to vote. I'm for her," I said.

"Me too," Peggy said.

"That makes it unanimous," Dad said. "I feel we should give you a medal, Carol, for putting up with this interrogation. Now if you two will go upstairs and get dressed, then maybe—"

"One second," Carol Gulden said, a mischievous little smile playing on her lips. "I wish someone would ask me if I still want to live here now that I know all these things about you."

"All what things?" we asked.

"Well, that you don't go to church, that all Robby cares about is sports, that Peggy is a born prosecutor and will probably ask me tough questions as long as I live here. This doesn't look like any bed of roses to me. This may not be the right place for me."

"We're pretty bad, but not that bad," I said. "Besides, roses have thorns."

"Please take the job," Peggy begged. "Dad'll pay you lots of money in addition to room and board."

"That's right," I said. "He paid Mrs. O'Rourke a hundred dollars a week back home. He'll pay you at least that much here."

Dad winced.

Carol laughed.

"As a matter of fact, we really haven't talked about money in addition to room and board," Dad said. "However, I am prepared to pay you four hundred and fifty dollars a month. The extra fifty is hardship pay for living with Peggy and Robby."

"That doesn't sound like enough," Carol replied with a straight face. "But I'll accept anyway."

"Whoopee," Peggy and I shouted. I thought Dad would have liked to shout too.

Carol moved in that afternoon. She got all her clothes in her VW in one trip. But it took us two trips to bring over all her books, papers, typewriter. I say "us" because I went over to the place she was living and helped bring her stuff down.

"You read even more than our mom did."

We were carrying loose books to the car. I tried to convince her it would be more efficient to box them, but she wanted to carry them loose and throw them on the backseat.

"What was your mom's name, Robby?" she asked me as we drove over to our house.

"Alice."

"When did she die?"

I liked how she asked that. Grown-ups usually say "pass away," and once I heard a neighbor in Watertown ask Dad when he lost his wife, as though he'd misplaced Mom in a Star Market.

"Two years ago. I was nine."

"That's hard," she said.

"She had cancer. We didn't know it till the end. I mean Peg and me. Peggy's nice really. She sounds tough. Heck, she really is tough, but she's nice. Did she embarrass you at all with her questions?"

"Not really. Nor did you."

"I like how you talk, Carol."

"What do you mean?"

"The way you just said 'nor did you.' It's kind of like you're writing it."

She looked at me. "You're not just a ballplayer, are you?"

"What do you mean?"

"You've got a good ear, and you think about what you hear. Well, I have a confession. Nobody asked me about it this morning so it didn't come up. I like to write. I write short stories and poems. I always wanted to be a professional writer. I knew it was hard to make a living writing, so I got a teacher's certificate, thinking I'd write after school."

She laughed. She had a merry laugh. "But there wasn't much chance of that. Teaching fourth grade was like having two full-time jobs. A principal I knew once said teaching elementary school was like having an open vein."

"What's that mean?"

"It means the school day never ends."

"Is that why you didn't get married? No time?"

She laughed. "No. As a matter of fact, I was hoping someone would come along and marry me and save

106

me from the fourth grade. But no one ever did."

"Maybe someone will. You're pretty."

She turned red. "Here we are," she said with a little embarrassed laugh. I could tell we hadn't got here a moment too soon.

That night Carol cooked her first meal for us, and it was terrific. Lamb chops, squash, salad, and for dessert she made a peach pie because, she told us, Michigan peaches are the best in the world.

While we were eating dessert she did a lot of bragging on Michigan, and we bragged a lot about Massachusetts. A lot of hot air was flowing back and forth, and Dad was enjoying it and throwing in his two cents for California when we heard the front door being unlocked.

Everyone stopped talking. "Who could that be?" Dad said, getting up from the table.

I knew right away who it could be. The only person who had a key to our house besides us. Mrs. Lowenfeld.

Peggy's eyes and mine met. Carol just looked puzzled. No one had told her about Mrs. Lowenfeld.

It was her all right. In a matching sweater and slacks and carrying a grocery bag.

"Hello, everyone," she called out. "Harry and I got done early with our clients, and I thought I'd bring you a kitchen warming present. It's just some bread and salt. An old Eastern European tradition."

She put the bag down on the counter and surveyed us with approval. "You all look as though you've lived here forever. And you, my dear, must be Carol Gulden. No, please don't get up. I'm Ruth Lowenfeld. A family friend. My, doesn't that peach pie look delicious."

"Carol made it," Peggy said.

"Warren, you *are* in luck."

Dad smiled. "Ruth, if it hadn't been for your ad in the paper we wouldn't have Carol or this pie. Why don't you sit down and have some with us."

Peggy and I glanced at each other.

"I'd love to, but I can't. Beth has a soccer game at the park right now, and I promised her that if I got through early I would show up for it. Not that I want to. Art's there, of course, and that is never pleasant."

She looked at me thoughtfully.

"Robby, how would you like to come over to the park with me and see Beth play?"

For a second I was about to say, Thanks but no thanks. I don't want to go anywhere with you. (I wouldn't have put it that way exactly.) But suddenly I realized this could be the perfect opportunity to meet Mr. Lowenfeld. Away from the world of computer programming. It would be a chance for me to see if he was the right kind of person for my plan to work. Mrs. Lowenfeld was doing me a big favor.

"Sure. I'd like to see her play."

"Can I come too?" Dad asked. "In fact, why don't we all come, unless you think it would make Beth nervous."

108

Mrs. Lowenfeld laughed. "Nothing makes that child nervous when it comes to sports."

"Carol, what about you?"

"Thank you, Mr. Miller," Carol said politely, "but I'd like to clean up, and then I've got some letters to write."

"I'll stay and help Carol," Peggy said.

"That's nice of you, Peggy, but I can manage alone."

"I know you can, but I *like* doing dishes."

What was Peg up to?

Carol laughed. "It's only loading the dishwasher."

"But I love loading dishwashers," Peggy said.

She was definitely cooking up something, and it had nothing to do with the kitchen.

Dad looked amused. "Never look a gift horse in the mouth, Carol. I think it's great Peggy wants to help in the kitchen. Just don't get in Carol's way, Peg."

"Oh, Dad," Peggy said so good-naturedly that I wondered that Dad didn't suspect something. But he didn't. Love is blind; it also makes you foolish.

"Can I meet you there?" I asked Mrs. Lowenfeld. "I'd like to go now."

I didn't like the idea of going there with them and having them close by when I got introduced to Mr. Lowenfeld.

"Let's the three of us go together," Dad said.

He was hooked, line and sinker. He wanted me and Mrs. Lowenfeld to hang around together. To get to know each other. Like each other.

Well, it was a big park, and I'd find a way to get away from both of them. I felt a little guilty having these private thoughts, sort of undermining Dad's plans. But his plans were for his happiness, mine was for our survival.

Late that night, in her room, Peg told me what happened between her and Carol.

"I thought you had a plan going at the table with all that phony talk about loving to do the dishes."

Peggy laughed. "No, I really just wanted to be alone with Carol. I wanted to ask her advice about Mrs. Lowenfeld. What she thought we could do about her."

"What'd she say?"

"She pretended she didn't know what I was talking about."

"She just couldn't believe anyone would start gossiping so fast about someone."

"Exactly," Peg said, unashamed. "She was loading the dishwasher, and I said, 'You can be honest, Carol. Robby and I hate that woman's guts.'

"Carol laughed and said, 'Peggy, those are pretty strong words. Why do you dislike her?'

" 'Hate, Carol, hate.'

" 'All right, hate. Would you hand me the dishwasher detergent?'

111

" 'I hate her because she wants to take over our family. She wants to marry Dad.'

" 'And how do you know that?'

" 'It's obvious. She brought us out here to Michigan. She rented this house for us. She kept a front-door key. She told us where to eat last night. She's got her hooks out for Dad.' "

"Wrong," I interrupted Peg's recital. "She's got her hooks *into* Dad."

"They're not into Dad until he proposes and she says yes."

"Which could be any moment now."

"I know. Anyway. Carol looked very uncomfortable. She started sweeping the floor and saying things like I was exaggerating and stuff like that, and finally she admitted that that was how a lot of men finally got married. 'And happily too,' she said.

"So I said, 'Our dad won't be happy with her. He'll be unhappy the rest of his life. You're a hundred times more like our mom than Mrs. Lowenfeld ever will be.'

"And that, Robby, was when I got my great idea."

Peggy started pacing the room. Quietly, because Dad was in his room and Carol was downstairs.

"What was your great idea?"

"That Dad should marry Carol."

I stared at her. "Are you nuts?"

"No. We've really been selfish, Robby. Last night at the restaurant, you remember him saying he was lonely. We've never thought about that, Robby. Dad's

112

still young. He should marry again. And wouldn't it be better if we helped him marry someone *we* liked too?''

I tried not to laugh. Only a girl who read a lot of romantic books would come up with a plan like this. My plan was so much more realistic. But I didn't dare tell it to Peg. Not the way she ran her mouth.

"Robby, Carol would be a perfect match for Dad. She's pretty. She's nice. She can cook. She's got a sense of—''

"Stop already. I don't want to throw cold water on your plan, but don't they have to fall in love with each other?''

"I've started working on that already. I asked Carol what she thought of Dad.''

"What'd she say?''

"She said she thought he was very nice.''

I laughed. "What else could she say? You want my honest opinion? It won't work.''

"I think it will.''

"And even if it does. Even if Dad falls in love with her and she falls in love with Dad. Then what? They get married. She becomes our stepmother, and maybe that's okay and maybe that's not, but we're still stuck here in Arborville . . .''

And then, like a dummy, I ran my mouth. . . .

"I've got a plan that will not only get Mrs. Lowenfeld out of our life but get us back to Massachusetts where we belong. And if Carol wants to move to Massachusetts with us, that's okay with me.''

113

She stopped pacing the room and sat down on her bed. "What's your plan?"

Suddenly, a little late, I got cautious.

"I . . . uh . . . can't talk about it now."

"You don't have a plan."

"I do."

"Well, it can't be any good or you'd tell me what it is."

I had to tell her something. I decided I'd give her enough to satisfy her, enough to get her off my back. And maybe she'd stop pumping me.

"You remember me and Dad and Mrs. Lowenfeld went to the park after supper to see Beth play."

She nodded.

"Well, guess who I met there?"

"Beth."

"C'mon, Peg, we've met Beth already. I met her dad. Mr. Lowenfeld. He's the soccer coach. It's why she doesn't like to go to Beth's games. It's also probably why she wanted me to go with her. So she'd have someone to talk to."

"What was he like?"

"He's a nice guy."

"Tell me what happened."

"We drove over in her sports car."

"I bet you liked that part."

"I didn't. It's a two-seater with room in back for one piece of luggage."

"And you were the luggage."

"Right."

"So?"

I relived the scene for her and for myself.

There were college kids playing softball, touch football, basketball. All the tennis courts were taken, and there was the big soccer game.

It was a blue team against a red one. The Sampson Park kids, Beth and the others, were in red shirts. Both sidelines were crowded with parents and little brothers and sisters and subs, and there was a lot of noise.

"There's Beth," Mrs. Lowenfeld said.

"Where?" Dad asked.

"She's got the ball now."

That was Beth? I couldn't believe it. From this distance she looked like a boy. She certainly moved like a guy. She was dribbling the ball off her toe, moving easily. A kid came up to tackle her (as they say in soccer), and she deked him (as we say in hockey)—feinting one way and sweeping past him the other—as neatly as I ever deked a kid on ice.

She was good. Real good.

They call soccer "football" in Europe, where it's a big sport, the way it is in South America. But as far as I'm concerned, soccer is a lot more like hockey than it is like our football. You play position on attack and you stick with your wing on defense. True, we never played soccer as an organized sport back home, but you could see that played correctly it ran on the same principles as hockey.

115

There was Beth dribbling through the forwards, or wings, and drawing the defense to her like bears to honey. Teddy bears. Just as two kids came up to block her, without breaking stride she booted the ball across to the other wing, a dark-haired kid who stopped it neatly, took two big steps and booted a hard shot into the near corner of the goal. The goalie never had a chance.

Right away the kid who scored started running around with his index fingers in the air yelling and jumping up and down, and in two seconds his teammates descended on him and banged him on the back and hugged him. The parents were all cheering—at least Beth's team's parents were cheering—and Beth was congratulating the kid too, but the one who had made the goal possible was Beth.

Sure as shooting, Mrs. Lowenfeld said the wrong thing.

"Beth should have kept the ball. She had a wonderful shot."

"She made a great pass," I said.

"I know, but Bobby de Vito will get all the credit."

So that was de Vito from the baseball team. And then I spotted the others—Joe Dawkins and Tom Tomzik and Kosmowski and Littlefield. They were all there.

Play started again. And now the Sampson Park team was on defense. Beth ran alongside her wing, keeping one eye on him and the other on the ball. A long kick toward her forward skipped by him and went out of bounds right near us. The ref's whistle blew. He pointed to the blue team's goal. Beth got the ball not far from us.

"I'm here, dear," Mrs. Lowenfeld called out.

Beth shot a quick look at her and saw us. She nodded and then threw an easy roller toward one of her defensemen, and then cut back upfield, hoping to get a return pass. The defenseman took it upfield himself.

"Spread out, red team," a man shouted from the other side of the field.

"Isn't that Art?" Dad asked.

"Yes," Mrs. Lowenfeld said grimly. "He wasn't interested in sports in California. He only coaches now so he can have extra time with her."

So that was Mr. Lowenfeld in the flesh. Tall, dark-haired, wearing a baseball cap. I wondered what excuse I could use to go around the field and talk to him.

"That's it, Joe," Mr. Lowenfeld shouted. "Bring it up, babe."

He had a nice way of yelling, I thought. Some coaches can split wood with their voices.

Joe Dawkins had the ball on his toe and was dribbling awkwardly. A blue team player came up and kicked the ball away from him. Joe was a lot better at football than at soccer.

"That's okay. Get back now," Mr. Lowenfeld shouted.

"I know his coaching shouldn't irritate me. It's

117

nice for Beth to have her father coaching," Mrs. Lowenfeld went on. "It makes it easier on her if some of those boys start teasing her, but he's doing it for the wrong reasons, Warren. By terms of the settlement we alternate weekends with Beth. This is supposed to be my weekend. If we were still married, he wouldn't even come to the games. He's cheating. There's no other word for it."

It was good to know Mr. Lowenfeld wasn't above cheating. That was essential to my plan.

"Can I go over to the other side, Dad? There's a kid I met the other day there I'd like to say hello to."

It was true. Mort Winkelman was on the sideline.

"All right, Robby, but keep an eye on us. I'm not sure how long we'll be staying."

It was great, their not wanting to go with me. There was no way she would want to greet her ex-husband. When things fall into place like that, you know you've got a very good plan.

I ran around the field behind the red team's parents and came up alongside Winkelman. He was watching the game.

"How're you doin', man?" I asked.

"Miller! Hey, Mr. Lowenfeld, here's the new guy we were telling you about."

"Later, Wink," Mr. Lowenfeld said. "Come on, Chester, you can't be that tired. Cut him off, George. Thata boy! We need that ball, kids. Go get it. There's not much time left."

There was less time than he thought.

118

The ref's whistle blew. A groan went up from the parents on our sideline.

"Is that it?" I asked Winkelman.

"Yeah. We lost again."

"All right, all right," Mr. Lowenfeld called out, and clapped his hands. "Let's congratulate them. They played well."

The two teams shook hands. Mr. Lowenfeld crossed the field and shook the other coach's hand. Then he walked back to this sideline, one arm around a kid and the other around Beth. She looked grim. She hated to lose. More than her father did, it looked like.

"What happens now?" I asked Winkelman.

"Team meeting. What we did wrong. You sure you want to play on this team?"

"Yes," I lied.

"It's your funeral. Hey, Mr. Lowenfeld, this is the new guy from Massachusetts. He's a good soccer player."

"No, I'm not," I started to say, and then stopped. He'd find that out for himself soon enough, and that wasn't important anyway.

"What's your name, son?" Mr. Lowenfeld asked me.

His face was as friendly in real life as it had been on the shelf in Beth's room.

"Robby Miller," Beth said. "That's him."

"Well, for goodness' sakes," he said, and laughed, and stuck out his hand. "You're Warren Miller's son."

"Yes, sir."

"Is your dad here now?"

I pointed to the other sideline.

"Of course," he said and gave a sort of half smile. Dad and Mrs. Lowenfeld were standing close together. "Well, as soon as we're done meeting I'll go over and say hello."

By now the whole team was gathered around. Tom Tomzik winked at me.

"Listen, kids," Mr. Lowenfeld said, "we didn't play all that badly. That number six of theirs was a good player. But we get another crack at them. This week we'll work on our passing. Spreading the field. We're still bunching up. How about Wednesday afternoon at five?"

"School starts Wednesday, Mr. Lowenfeld," someone said.

"It doesn't run till five. Okay, kids, we'll get this one back. Beth!"

The meeting was over. Parents came over and started talking to their kids. Joe Dawkins, Winkelman, Tom Tomzik, looked at me questioningly, but I shook my head. I was going to stick with Mr. Lowenfeld for a while.

Mr. Lowenfeld smiled at me and Beth. "Well, shall the three of us go over and shake hands like civilized folks?"

The way he said that told me that he didn't want to go alone. He wanted the protection of little kids. That could only mean one thing. He was still in love with his wife. How a nice guy like him could be in love with someone like her was beyond me, but it was good for my plan. Mr. Lowenfeld would do anything to remarry his wife, and Beth would do anything to help him.

Things were falling into place.

"So then what happened?" Peggy asked.

"We got together. He and Dad shook hands and everyone pretended they were glad to see each other."

"What about him and *her?*"

I laughed. "Not so friendly on her part. She had found out about the soccer practice for Wednesday. She said Beth had a piano lesson Wednesday. He said he thought her piano lessons were on Thursdays, and she said no, Wednesdays this year, and he said he'd change the practice to Tuesday then. That was when I asked him for a tryout.

" 'You're a soccer player, son?'

"I wished Dad wasn't there, because I would have lied and said, 'Yes, a good one.' But Dad knew soccer wasn't my sport. So all I said was, 'I play at it.' Well, he thought I was being real modest and therefore I must be great.

" 'Tell you what,' he said. 'Beth and I'll give you a tryout tomorrow right here.'

"Of course, right away, Mrs. Lowenfeld was sore.

'Why do you need Beth for that?' she asked him.

" 'I need someone for him to kick the ball to,' he said. 'And someone to kick the ball to him.'

" 'Why can't *you* do it?'

" 'Because I've got to watch him. You can't coach and play at the same time, Ruth. And it's too late to get someone else. Beth's here; she's good; she's willing.' A little smile came across his face. 'I'd think you'd want Warren's boy to have a crack at making the team, Ruth.' "

"He had her there," Peggy said.

"And don't you think she didn't know it. She was furious, but there wasn't much she could do about it. Not in front of Dad. She shrugged and said it was okay with her."

"Talk about soccer games," Peggy said. "They're just kicking Beth back and forth between them. So what's your plan, Robby?"

She hadn't forgot.

"All I can tell you, Peg, is that it involves Mr. Lowenfeld."

"How?"

"I can't tell you."

"Why not? I told you my plan."

I was silent. Suddenly I wasn't sure whether I was keeping mum because I feared she'd blab or because I was kind of ashamed of what my plan involved.

"I'll tell you if it works."

She smiled superiorly. "You don't have a plan, little brother, do you? Really?"

Maybe this was the best way out. I smiled and shook my head.

"I thought so. Well, I think Carol's the answer to Mrs. Lowenfeld, and I'm going to work on it. Now get out of here. I'm going to sleep. Hand me that book."

Peggy was like Mom. Neither of them could go to sleep without a book in their hands.

I handed her a book sitting on top of an unpacked carton. The name of it was *Hallie's Luck*.

"Any good?"

"You wouldn't like it."

"What's it about?"

"A girl who wants a boy to notice her, but he won't."

"What does she do?"

"So far all she's done is hit him with a rock."

"Boy, if a girl did that to me, I'd notice her all right. With a big fat lip."

"I don't think there's any girl around who'd want you to notice her."

I laughed. Peggy always gets the last word. "Good night, Peg."

"Good night, Robby. And don't worry about Dad. I think he's going to like Carol a lot. And I think she likes him already."

I didn't say anything. It sounded like Peggy had watched one soap opera too many. It was funny when you thought about it. Here we were: me, Peg, and Beth Lowenfeld, three kids involved in this mess, and each of us had our own plan. Peggy's was the dumbest. Beth's was the most unrealistic. She kept thinking if she brought her folks together—like at the game today—they'd stay together. Well, her father wanted to, obviously, but not Mrs. Lowenfeld.

My plan was the best, even though I felt like a traitor. If everything fell into place, Mr. Lowenfeld could have his company back, Mrs. Lowenfeld wouldn't have Dad, and maybe then Beth could get her folks together. Mr. Lowenfeld was the right kind of person for me, too. He was a nice guy, but he obviously wasn't above cheating a little. I mean here he was coaching and calling special practices for the wrong reason. To have more time with his daughter. Well, my plan could give him that all right.

"What are you thinking about, Robby?" Peggy asked.

"Nothing."

"Close the door behind you, please."

I shut the door and went to the bathroom. There was a light on in Dad's study. I could hear the quiet whirr of his computer. And, if I listened by the door (which I did), the clicks of his keyboard. The clicks stopped.

"Who's that?" he called softly.

"Me."

"Robby, it's almost midnight." He opened the door. "What are you doing up?"

"I'm going to bed now."

"Is Peggy up too?"

"She's reading."

"Come in for a second." He shut the door behind

me. I looked at his computer. The screen was filled with figures. It could be anything. I'd have to go by the labels on the disks.

"Robby, I hope and believe that when school starts you and Peggy will fall into a routine and you'll stop worrying so much about Ruth Lowenfeld."

"Sure," I said, looking at his disks.

"Right now neither of you have enough on your minds."

"You're right, Pop." When he was done he'd probably put the disks in his file.

"I'm really more worried about Peggy than you. Right now Peggy is scheming to have me fall in love with our student housekeeper downstairs. I wish she'd find other things to think about."

"I'm sure she will." I looked at the figures on the screen, wondering if they would make sense to Mr. Lowenfeld. Of course they would. They had to.

"I hope you're not scheming something, Robby."

Startled, I looked at him. "Just how to make friends."

He smiled. "That will happen soon enough. It's very nice of Art Lowenfeld to give you a special tryout. Did you like him?"

"Yeah. He's a nice guy."

"I think so too. Perhaps a bit too disorganized to be a success in business, but he's very intelligent and he's very nice."

"Did you ever find out why they got divorced?"

Dad smiled and shook his head. "My suspicion, son, is that they were never really well mated, and

126

time simply ran out on their marriage."

I hadn't the slightest idea what that meant, and thought I'd gone far enough. "Good night, Dad."

"Good night, Robby."

We looked at each other. He wanted to kiss me, I knew. And I wanted to kiss him, but neither of us could bust out of our shells. Besides, if I kissed him, it would be really two-faced. What I was going to do was awful, but I had no choice if I was going to save us.

I went into the bathroom and brushed my teeth. The light was out in Peggy's room. I got into my pajamas and into bed, and lay there looking at the ceiling and listening to the noises of our new house.

All houses breathe their own ways at night. In California, our houses had squeaked in the family rooms for some reason.

In Massachusetts, our house in Malden had squeaked in the kitchen. So badly that Dad spent hours looking for mouse droppings before he finally gave up and decided it was layers of linoleum over old wooden floors over a shifting foundation over deep movements in the earth's crust. Engineers like to get to the bottom of things.

We never got rid of the squeaks in Malden.

In Watertown, it was our basement that made noises. The wind, not to mention mice, came through cracks in the concrete walls. As a result our basement in Watertown sort of whistled in the night. It always amazed me though that you could never hear a house make noises in the daytime.

Here, in Arborville, I could tell it was going to be those old oak stairs talking at night. They squeaked as though ghosts of past owners and renters were going up and down them.

But I didn't really believe in ghosts. When you died you died. I've known that for some time.

Once when Mom was very sick and I was crying a lot, she tried to comfort me.

"But I don't want you to die," I wept.

I didn't even know what death meant. All it was to me was a bad word. Mom put her arms around me and took me into bed with her and said everything was going to be all right no matter what happened. That people were born and people died and we were all part of the earth—cats, dogs, trees, flowers, rivers, rain. And no one ever really went away. She talked to me a long time, and I fell asleep in her arms.

Now Mom was in a coffin under the ground, and I don't know about the trees and the flowers and the rivers and the rain. I don't know about death. Mom really went away.

I started to cry. I hadn't cried in over a year, but now I was crying again. I buried my face in the pillow so no one could hear me.

I could tell it was Sunday morning even before I was awake. It was the smell of bacon frying that did it. And I could hear music playing on the radio downstairs. That's the way it always was with Sunday.

Plus on Sundays we always ate breakfast in the dining room with a tablecloth and freshly cut flowers. Mom cut the flowers. Mom was a great one for ritual. Dad tried hard to keep it up, but first the flowers went and then the tablecloth and then the special breakfasts, so that after a few months we ate Sunday breakfast the way we ate weekday breakfasts. Everyone on his own—cereal and toast and whatever met your eye.

There was one other thing Mom did for Sunday breakfast. She squeezed fresh oranges. Well, I couldn't smell the orange juice, but I sure could smell the bacon, and I bet the flowers were there too. Sunday. Mom.

I got goose pimples. I jumped out of bed and ran to the top of the stairs.

"What's going on?" I shouted down the old staircase. I was holding on to the banister for dear life.

Carol came out of the kitchen. She was wearing a blue-and-white apron with flowers on it.

"What's going on, young man, is that you finally woke up. Your father and sister have eaten and gone. I've eaten, and in five minutes I'm going, too. Come on down. Your bacon's getting a bit crispy."

I shook my head. What had I been thinking! I took a deep breath and went downstairs.

"You're a real sleeper, aren't you?" Carol said.

I peered into the dining room. The table was set with a tablecloth. There were cut flowers on the table.

"Who told you to do that? Whose idea was that? To eat in the dining room, the flowers . . . the bacon? Was that Peggy's idea?"

Carol looked at me puzzled. "No. It was mine. In our home we always ate Sunday breakfast in the dining room. And we had flowers from the garden when there were flowers from the garden to be had. Is there something wrong with that?"

"Yes," I heard myself say, "I don't like it."

"Oh? Peggy did. She said your mother always put out flowers too. And your father didn't mind. I'm sorry you don't approve. Now if you'll tell your humble housekeeper how you want your eggs, Master Robert, she will go and prepare them for you. There's also freshly squeezed orange juice in the fridge."

I stared at her. "I don't believe you."

"What don't you believe?"

130

"That Peggy didn't put you up to this."

"Put me up to what?"

I shook my head. I couldn't say it.

"All right, Robby, how do you want your eggs?"

"I don't want eggs. I want cereal."

"Good. Cereal is probably healthier for you. You'll find Rice Krispies and Special Ks in the cupboard over the bread box. As soon as I get the dishwasher loaded I'll be off. I get Sundays off, Master Robert."

She was real funny with that Master Robert stuff. She didn't know me that well that she should be so sarcastic with me.

And I didn't know her that well that I should have asked her my next question. But I did. I had too.

"Are you going to church, too?" I asked her. Mom was the only one in our family who went to church regularly.

"No," she said, not taking offense. "I'm going to bike to the university library. . . . Peggy has lent me her bike, and then if it's still nice out, I'm going to bike down to the river. And after that I don't know what I'm going to do. I may go to a movie. But I assure you, young man, in case you don't know it, there's going to be a life for Carol Gulden outside of this house."

"Okay. I'm sorry to be so grumpy. . . . It's just that . . ." I still couldn't find the words. Or maybe I could find them but didn't want to say them.

"It's just what, Robby?" she asked, and her voice was kindly. I gritted my teeth. Was she trying to make

131

me cry again? There was no way she could live with us. She was too much like Mom. It was *bad*.

I cleared my throat. "What time is it anyway?"

"Almost eleven." She went into the kitchen. I followed her. "What time did you go to bed last night?"

"Late. Where did Dad and Peg go?"

"They went out to buy telephones."

"On Sunday?"

"Yes. You can buy anything you want on Sunday except liquor. I think they're also planning to look for furniture later on today." She shut the dishwasher door. "When you're done would you put your dishes in here?"

"Sure."

She looked at me standing there in the doorway of the kitchen.

"Why don't you go up and put on a bathrobe, Robby? It's Sunday."

I stared at her. There was no other way she would have known to say that. Peggy had told her. That and everything else too: the bacon, the flowers, the tablecloth, the orange juice. It was part of Peggy's plot to get Dad to fall in love with her. Mom had never let us eat in our pajamas. Sunday mornings we always got dressed or wore bathrobes.

That got me so angry. "I want to tell you something, Carol."

"Yes?"

"You're not my mom."

"What did you say?"

"I said, 'You're not my mom.' And you won't ever be."

Her face turned red. "I don't know what you're talking about, Robby," she said. "I don't want to be your mom. And if my suggesting to you that you eat in your bathrobe provoked that, then as far as I'm concerned, you can eat naked. I'm going now."

She left. A few moments later, I heard the back door open and close. I went into the dining room and watched Carol go down the driveway on Peggy's bike. She had on a backpack. I guess full of books. The bike wobbled a bit. Peggy was crazy to lend her her bike. She'd wreck it, sure as shooting.

I felt bad watching her bike off down the street. Maybe I'd made a mistake accusing her like that. Maybe Peggy hadn't told her. Maybe it was all natural, her being like Mom.

Well, there was nothing I could do about it now. I went into the kitchen and took a glass of the freshly squeezed orange juice out of the fridge and carried it upstairs. I'd change, put on a bathrobe, and eat the way Mom wanted me to eat on Sunday mornings.

That was what I was going to do, but I didn't do it. By the time I reached the top of the stairs, it hit me that I had the house to myself for the first time. If I was going to put my plan into action, now was the time.

I went into Dad's study and drank the juice and looked around.

It had to be in one of his disk files. I put the glass

133

down on his desk and opened a file. It was filled with blank disks. Well, I'd need a blank disk. In another box I found a DOS—data operating system—disk. So far so good. Now I had to find a REXCOMP disk.

That wasn't as easy. I was hoping it would be in plain sight since he was working on that program. But Dad, being a careful man and a creature of habit, wouldn't leave anything so important in plain sight— even in his own house.

I went through one box of disks after another. No REXCOMP label on any of them. I was going through his drawers when I heard a car slow down outside. I ran across the hall and into my room. I looked out the window. It was a strange car, and it kept going— looking for a different house number. I relaxed and went back to the study.

Could he have taken it with him? That didn't make sense. He would keep the original at his office. He wouldn't keep the copy with the original. I opened up every drawer in sight, all the time knowing he wouldn't keep a disk in a drawer. Then, finally, in desperation I went where I'd never gone before—into Dad's briefcase—and there I found it, on the top of some papers: a floppy disk with REXCOMP in Dad's handwriting on the label.

Okay. This was it. Last chance to back out. This was the bridge you crossed when you came to it. Now I was at it. If I crossed it, I was doing something wrong. I was breaking the law. I was stealing one of Dad's computer programs. Stealing an idea, which is as bad as stealing money.

I hesitated. You've got to do it, I thought. There's no way you can have her for a mother. You're doing it for Peg, too. And you're doing it for Dad's sake too, even though he may not realize. And if it comes off, there's even a chance Mr. and Mrs. Lowenfeld will get together again, and that will make Beth happy too. You're doing this for everyone.

Still, I hesitated. My head ached. Good and bad were mixed up inside me. I stared at the computer. It was plugged in. It was always plugged in. The tiny red surge protector light was on—a familiar reassuring glow. Our night-light.

I took a deep breath. Here goes nothing, I thought. I went to work.

I put the DOS disk in the A drive and hit the switch. The old familiar and reassuring whirring noise that I associated with Dad came on. You could hear it late at night if you woke up. And if you got up and went to the bathroom, you could see, through the half-open door, Dad sitting there peering at the screen. It might be three in the morning, and he'd still be working. Lost in his work.

I got rid of the date and time on the screen and typed the disk copy command.

The computer screen told me to put the source disk in A drive and the destination disk in B drive. I took out the DOS disk and slipped the REXCOMP disk into the A drive and the blank disk into B. Then I hit ENTER to start copying the program.

Lights started blinking between the two drives. A message on the screen told me the disk was being formatted. In a couple of seconds the copying would start. You always think of computers being a fast way to do things, but this felt slow.

When the message flashed saying it was copying, I got up and went back across the hall and looked out my window. Nothing happening. No cars moving. Good. The machine was clicking in Dad's study. In a minute it would be done. I was in luck so far. That was what I was thinking when I saw our station wagon coming up the street.

I ran back. The computer was still whirring. The red lights were still blinking back and forth between the drives. Come on, come on! Move it! MOVE IT! I felt like a coach.

Outside I heard our station wagon pull up in our driveway.

The whirring stopped. An amber message appeared on the screen:

DISK COPIED. DO YOU WANT TO COPY
ANOTHER ONE? STRIKE Y FOR YES.
STRIKE N FOR NO.

I heard the car doors open. I hit N. The pulsating lights went on again.

I heard the front door open.

I reached down to the surge protector and turned off the power. Not the proper way to quit the program, but there was no time to do it the proper way.

"Robby, are you awake yet?" Dad called up the stairs.

"He's got to be awake by now," Peggy said.

"He was up very late," Dad said.

"I don't care. I can't believe he's still sleeping," Peggy said. "I'm going to wake him up."

"I'll do it," Dad said.

I put the DOS disk back in his file on the shelf, the REXCOMP disk back in his briefcase, and with disk copy in hand I tiptoed back to my room and closed my door. They hadn't seen me. Thank goodness for a big house. I put the disk in my closet under a pile of clothes. Not the best place to store a floppy disk. Still, no one would ever think of looking for it there. Then I hopped back into bed just as there was a knock on my door.

"Robby," Dad said softly.

I didn't answer. I breathed in and out regularly.

The door opened. "He's faking," Peggy said. "I can tell."

I opened my eyes, blinking hard. Dad was standing there with a phone in his hand.

"What time is it?" I asked, putting sleep into my voice.

"It's almost noon," Dad said. "Do you feel all right?"

"You weren't sleeping," Peggy said.

"Late hours aren't good for you, son. Come on, it's time to get up. Carol's left breakfast for you. There's freshly squeezed orange juice, bacon—"

137

"She even put flowers on the dining-room table," Peggy said. "Like Mom used to do. She's really nice, isn't she, Dad?"

"Did you tell her to do that?" I said.

"No. Did I, Dad?"

Dad shook his head. "Her family seems to have had the same customs we had. She's a very nice girl."

"She's not a girl," Peggy said. "She's a woman, and not much younger than you."

"All right, Peggy," Dad said. He turned to me. "As soon as I install the phones, Peggy and I are going out to a furniture place and look for chairs for the living room and an easy chair for Carol's room. Do you want to come along?"

"I can't. I've got a soccer tryout."

"So you do. Well, you better hurry along or you'll be late for that. Peggy can help you get breakfast."

"I can help myself," I said, getting out of bed.

"You weren't sleeping, were you?" Peggy asked the moment Dad was out of the room.

I shook my head.

"So what's going on, little brother?"

I stepped carefully over the pile of clothes on the floor of my closet and reached for a pair of pants and a shirt.

"Nothing."

"You're not telling the truth."

"Peggy," Dad called, "were you in my study?"

"No," Peggy said.

"There's an empty juice glass here."

Peggy shot me a look. I shook my head. Not now, I was silently telling her. I'll explain later.

"And the disk I've been working on isn't in the file," Dad called.

I was about to say, "It's in your briefcase where you left it," but stopped myself in time.

"What *are* you up to, Robby?" Peggy whispered.

"I'll tell you later."

"Here it is in my briefcase. Good Lord, I'm getting old. But I still don't understand about the juice glass."

"You probably took it upstairs by accident," I said.

"I probably did at that," Dad said. Which was something he would never have done, since he had strict rules against eating or drinking around a computer.

In a second we heard him puttering with the modem and the phone. It was typical of Dad. The first phone he'd install in our new house would be his computer link to the Computel Company.

"Okay," Peggy said, "now tell me."

"I'll tell you downstairs. I'm getting dressed now."

I was stalling. I owed Peggy an explanation. For that matter I owed her my whole plan, but she could still blow it with one slip of the tongue. If she had a personality like Beth Lowenfeld's, a silent gum chewer, it would be different.

Peggy left my room reluctantly, and I got dressed . . . slowly. I was stalling while Dad was installing.

In the end we went down the stairs together.

Peggy gave me an irritated look. She knew that I couldn't talk in front of Dad.

"There's bacon and eggs, Robby," Dad said.

"I don't have time. I'll just have bacon and toast."

"That bacon looks pretty dried out," Dad said. "We better not let Carol see it. I think I ought to tell her I've got her telephone."

"She's not here. She took off on Peggy's bike. I think you were dumb to lend her your bike, Peg. She probably hasn't ridden a bike in a long time."

"How do you know she did that?" Dad asked.

"Did what?"

"That she borrowed Peggy's bike. I thought you were asleep."

I bit my lip. First the juice glass and now this. I thought fast.

"I woke up and looked out the window and saw her, and then I fell asleep again."

When you lie you stick to it even if it sounds ridiculous. In fact, sometimes the stupider it sounds the more people believe it. Like no one could make up something that dumb. I could tell Peggy knew I was lying right through my teeth. "Hey, I got to go. See you guys later," I said.

Before either of them could say anything, I hustled my dishes out of the dining room.

"We may be gone awhile on this furniture expedition," Dad called after me. "Don't get lost again. I don't want a repetition of two nights ago. We're having Sunday dinner at the Lowenfelds' at four-thirty.

140

I want you home by four, Robby."

"Sure, Dad."

I ran up the stairs.

"Now where are you going?"

"To put on good sneakers."

I didn't change sneakers. I got the disk out from under the clothes and wrapped it carefully in a sweatshirt. Then I tore down the stairs again. If there were an Olympic event for running down steps with a floppy disk, I'd have won the gold.

My cover was a soccer tryout.

And that was a laugh. Because I wasn't a soccer player. It would probably be as big a laugh as Dad's tale about his one and only high school football tryout. I remembered that story as I biked over to Sampson Park.

Dad wasn't an athlete. He never went out for sports . . . except once. It was on an army post in Wiesbaden, Germany.

The football coach had only sixteen kids come out, so he asked everyone on the base who had high-school-aged sons to tell them to come out for the football team. Grampa Miller was in command of the base, so Dad couldn't very well refuse. Family honor was at stake. So one cold, windy afternoon after school Dad stood on a football field in Germany with about a dozen other skinny, nonathletic army brats, all shivering in shorts and T-shirts. All of them feeling and looking miserable. (Dad's words.)

As Dad tells it, "The coach took one look at us and said, 'All right, let's do a little weeding.'

"He put one of us at one end of the field. And he had the starting eleven at the other end, and they kicked off to that one person, who was supposed to catch the ball and then try to run through the whole team."

"Without blocking?" I asked.

"Without anything. Not even shoulder pads."

"What was he trying to prove?"

"Who had guts and who didn't."

"What did you do?"

"When my turn came, I caught the ball and started running."

"How far did you get?"

"A lot farther than any of the other kids."

"Way to go. I bet Grampa was proud of you."

"Far from it," Dad said gravely. "You see, Robby, when I saw those eleven bruisers bearing down on me, shouting that they were going to tear my head off, I quite sensibly ran the other way."

"With the ball?"

"Of course with the ball. I pretended I didn't know how the game was played."

"Oh, Dad." I couldn't help laughing. "Did they catch you?"

"Only after I jumped into a jeep with the ball. They had a hard time tackling me in the jeep."

I laughed a lot. "What did Grampa say?"

"By the time the story reached him it had changed quite a bit . . . for the worse. I was supposed to have started the jeep and driven it around the base with the football team in hot pursuit. I became a legend of sorts for about a week. And for that week, I'm ashamed to say, your grandfather didn't speak to me. But I was a hero to others. In fact, right after I made my wrong way move with the ball, two others tried the same thing, but by then the jeep had been moved and they were tackled and piled on pretty hard."

"Boy, I hope no Russian spies were watching."

"If they were, some pretty optimistic reports must have been relayed back to Moscow about the youth of America. Anyway, that was my first and last sports tryout. Grampa never asked me to try out for anything again. He said it was bad for his career. But he would have been proud of you, though. Everywhere we've moved, you've tried out and made the team."

Grampa Miller died in a plane accident before I was born. Grandma Miller lives in Cape May, New Jersey, and we see her about once a year.

Dad was right about tryouts in the past. I'd made teams in Malden, Scituate, and Watertown. In Watertown, I'd made a hockey team and a baseball team. In a way, the other day in the park with Dawkins and Winkelman and Tom Tomzik, I'd already had a tryout for a football team and made it. The problem was there was no football team to make.

But there was a soccer team to make. There was

144

also no way I'd ever make it, but that, of course, wasn't why I was trying out.

On the field near the flagpole, there were some little kids kicking a soccer ball back and forth. But no Beth. I looked at my watch. It was just twelve. I was on time. I biked past the field holding the sweatshirt carefully.

At the basketball court a full-court game was going on with high school kids. There were also some little kids hitting a Wiffle ball over the roof of a sort of clubhouse near the basketball court.

Beth Lowenfeld saw me before I saw her. She had been watching the basketball game. A black-and-white soccer ball was under her arm.

I biked over to her.

"Dad said he was gonna be late," she said. "You wanna practice some?"

"Sure. Where?"

"Near the kiddies' pool. C'mon."

She got on her bike and I followed her. I couldn't bike as fast as she could because the ground was bumpy, and the last thing I needed was to have a floppy disk slip out of my sweatshirt.

"Here's good enough," she said. She hopped off her bike. I got off mine carefully. I set the sweatshirt down against a tree.

She waited, watching me. I guess she'd never seen anyone be that careful with an old sweatshirt.

"Okay?" she called out.

"Yeah."

She kicked the ball to me and I kicked it back, straight on with my toe the way I knew soccer-style football kickers didn't do it. She didn't say anything. All her kicks to me were low and hard. Mine were all over the place.

She stopped the ball with her toe and dribbled it over to me. I waited for her to try to deke me but she didn't try. She stopped the ball with her toe and looked at me.

"You're not a soccer player."

"I never said I was."

"We already got too many kids on our team. They're thinking of forming another team with the left-overs."

I laughed. "That'd be a great name for a team. The Sampson Park Leftovers."

She didn't smile. "You don't really care, do you?"

I shook my head. "Not about soccer." I took a deep breath. I was going to tell her now. It felt right. Natural. We were both working for the same thing: not letting her mom get involved with my dad.

"I only came here 'cause I want to talk to your father."

"What about?"

I got the sweatshirt and took the floppy disk out of it.

"This."

146

"What is it?" she asked.

"A floppy disk." I held it out to her, and she took it.

"I know that. What's on it?"

"A program he'd like to know about."

For a second she didn't say anything. Then she said, "Are you doing a bad thing?"

She really got to the heart of things.

"Not if it turns out to be good for all of us. It could get me and my dad and Peggy back to Massachusetts. And it could get your father and mother together again." I took a deep breath. "Give it to your father."

The words just fell out of my mouth. I hadn't planned it that way at all. I was gonna give it to Mr. Lowenfeld myself. In a way what I was doing was chicken. Sharing a bad thing, sharing the guilt.

"Just give it to him," I repeated.

She looked at the disk. She shook her head. "I won't do it."

"Hey, do you want *your* mother to marry *my* father?"

"No."

"I don't either. I've thought hard about this, Beth. There's only one way to stop that from happening. We've got to make sure the Computel Company fails. If that happens, your mom would be really upset with my dad, wouldn't she?"

"Yeah."

"And that would end their partnership, wouldn't it?"

"Probably."

"Take my word for it, it would. The company your dad works for—Block Electronics—it's gonna do a lot better, and your mother is gonna feel a lot better about your dad."

She was silent. Then she said, stubbornly, "It's wrong."

"Yeah, but so is your mother and my father getting married. That's very wrong. This way your folks'll get back together and we'll be back in Massachusetts, and that's right, not wrong."

A car horn tooted. We both looked. It was him. Mr. Lowenfeld. He waved to us. He was looking for a place to park. Beth was still holding the disk.

"I'm going. Tell him you found it in the grass and don't know what it is."

She opened her mouth to protest. I didn't give her a chance. I took off on my bike and started pedaling madly.

"What about the tryout?" she yelled at me.

She was a jock all right. "Tell him I was lousy," I shouted back. "It's the truth. Tell him I'm going to try out for the Sampson Park Leftovers and I probably won't make them, either."

She shouted something but I didn't hear it, because by then I was past the kiddies' pool, the monkey bars, and swings, past the soccer field and then down a walk and out of the park. Once I was on the street, I stopped pedaling and looked back. Mr.

Lowenfeld was talking to Beth. He had the disk in his hands.

I took off down the street. Toward our house. I hoped Dad and Peg were gone. I had just launched something big. I wanted to be alone for a while.

Our car was still there. I kept on pedaling.

Olivia dead-ended in a street called Hill Street. I turned to the right there. I looked at my watch. I'd only been gone about twenty minutes. Dad wanted me back by four. That only gave me four hours to kill.

I came up to a traffic light at Hill and Washtenaw. While I waited for the light to change, I wondered what Mr. Lowenfeld would do. He'd be curious to see what was on the disk. He'd go home or to his office and put the disk on a PC and check it out.

The rest was up to him. All I had to do now was kill time.

Killing time in a new town is kind of fun. You can explore.

It was a nice Sunday afternoon. There were students out and people walking with little kids. No kids my age hanging out though. I guess there was a church nearby, because people were walking all dressed up in their Sunday clothes. We used to wear Sunday clothes when Mom was alive.

There really was a hill on Hill Street. I was going downhill fast, winding around smoothly, shooting past a lot of big houses. I love going downhill fast around curves. You don't really steer with your handlebars, but with your body, leaning into each curve. A racer back in Watertown had taught me that.

Back home in Watertown on a swell day like this Monk and the guys were probably playing baseball or hanging out on their bikes arguing about the Sox and if they were going to choke again.

The streets back home would be filled with cars. Here in this fancy section I was biking in you couldn't even spot a stray cat. Wrong. Just as I coasted around a curve I spotted two adults jogging in the street ahead of me.

I shot by them. Faster and faster I went. The air tore at my face. After a couple more minutes of winding around, things began to open up. Fewer houses, more sky, and then suddenly I saw the river. Blue water, a bridge, little green islands.

I shot down toward the bridge, crossed it, and then, braking, I bounced over railroad tracks, turned right, and then was biking in some kind of riverside park. I guess this was where everyone in Arborville went on nice Sunday afternoons, because there were lots of folks here. And bike trails everywhere and little foot bridges over to the small islands. It was neat. Back home we had the Charles and the Mystic River, but no bike trails like this. Too many cars back home. Not enough room back home. The East was crowded.

151

Still, that was where home was.

The trail went along the riverbank. I cut around a family walking with fishing poles, buckets, and nets. There were bikers ahead of me. It was really nice, I have to admit.

I biked along one trail and then switched over to another, always keeping alongside the river. I saw ducks and model boats that were controlled electronically. There was a small playground with picnic tables and grills and water fountains. A guy was throwing a Frisbee to his dog. Couples walked arm in arm, people fished along the bank, and the river was filled with canoes and sailboats and windsurfers and even a couple of boats with little putt-putt trolling motors.

"Heads up!" A voice called behind me, and a guy in a helmet and on a racing bike shot by me as though I were standing still.

Five seconds later I saw Carol Gulden.

At first I wasn't sure it was her. There was a bench, and a bike near the bench. It was the bike I recognized first. It was Peggy's bike. Carol was sitting on the embankment below . . . reading. Naturally, she wouldn't use a bench. Mom wouldn't have either.

I pedaled off the trail and down the embankment toward her.

"Heads up!" I yelled. "This is my first time on a bike."

Carol jumped about three feet. I mean she practically levitated in a sitting position. I braked about six inches from her, laughing.

"You," she said.

"Scared you, didn't I?"

"To say the least. So you've discovered the river."

"Sure have. How do you like Peggy's bike?"

"Very much. Tomorrow I'm going to buy one."

"You could always borrow ours."

"Thanks, but I ought to have my own bike."

"You're not mad at me anymore, are you?"

"No. I wasn't really mad at you before. Just startled by your accusation."

"Sorry about that. It's just that when I got up and smelled the bacon frying, I had the craziest feeling that Mom was in the kitchen. And then everything else . . . the flowers, the music on the radio, the orange juice, the bathrobe business. It was too much."

Carol looked at me curiously. "I'm sorry," she said.

"Heck, it's okay. You couldn't've known." And then to change the subject: "What're you reading?"

"A novel."

"For school?"

She laughed. "No. For myself."

"Peg's a big reader. She reads for herself too. I only read for school. And Dad, he's the worst of us all. He won't read anything but computer stuff."

Carol put a piece of grass in her book and closed it.

"Hey," I said. "I didn't mean to interrupt you. I'll bike on."

"You're not interrupting me, Robby. Rivers are hard

153

to read by." She got up and started walking back to the bench where her backpack was.

"Back home you leave your backpack out like that . . . it's gone, man."

She smiled, and slipped her book inside it. "Yet you liked it back there?"

"You bet. The people were great."

She put the pack on and got on the bike. "When they weren't stealing your backpacks, you mean."

I laughed. "Hey, my friends don't steal. No one I know steals things."

Except me, I thought.

"Good. I'll see you later, Robby. Do you know how to get home?"

"Follow Hill Street."

"That's right. Do you know how to get to Hill Street from here?"

"It runs right into the river, doesn't it?"

"No. There are a few turns before that."

"You're kidding. I thought I followed Hill Street all the way down here."

"You couldn't have. Hill runs into Geddes, and then there's another street. Listen. When you go past the railroad tracks, make a right and then another right and then a left and—"

"I'll follow you home right now," I said.

And that's why I was home alone with Carol Gulden when Mr. Lowenfeld came to our house.

I followed Carol only till we got onto Hill Street, then I stood up on the bike pedaling hard and caught up with her. No one said it was a race home, but you know how those things are.

It wasn't really fair. I had a ten speed, and Peggy's bike was a three speed. Carol was puffing hard.

"I'll wait for you at the top of the hill," I said.

"Thanks a lot," she grunted.

She was a good sport all right, and after a while I stopped being a clown and we biked together. We didn't talk, because it was mostly uphill and Carol was out of shape.

I thought about Mr. Lowenfeld while we biked. He must have discovered by now what was on the disk. I didn't expect him to thank me. I expected him to make a copy of the disk and maybe give it back to Beth to give back to me. I wasn't sure how he'd work his end of the deal.

It took a lot longer going home than going to the

river. I guess that's always true. It's always downhill to a river. Our station wagon wasn't in the driveway. A look at my watch told me I'd been gone about an hour and a half. They'd still be a while furniture shopping. I could start unpacking some of the cartons in my rooms. Not all, as we'd only be packing to go back home in a little while. How long did I give us in Michigan? A month. Two at the outside.

"Thanks for the company, Robby," Carol said. We put our bikes in the garage.

"Thanks for leading me home. I couldn't have got here by myself."

Carol had a key to the back door.

"I'm going to shower, Robby, and then I'll be going out. See you later."

"You bet."

I went upstairs to my room. She was really nice. It wasn't going to be hard at all having her under the same roof. It probably wouldn't be such a bad thing if Dad fell in love with her and married her. She wasn't Mom, but she was as close to Mom as you could get. Dad could marry someone a lot worse all right.

If he married her and we all moved back to Water-town . . . that would be the best. Well, I was taking care of the Watertown part and Peggy was working on the marriage part, so maybe things would work out just like that. That's what I was thinking when the doorbell rang.

"I'll get it," I shouted. Which was kind of dumb,

since Carol couldn't have heard me, not to mention the doorbell, over the running water.

I opened the door. And there was Mr. Lowenfeld. My heart skipped a beat. In his hand was the floppy disk. I tried to keep my voice normal.

"Hi," I said, and smiled.

He wasn't smiling. "Your dad home, Robby?"

My knees almost buckled, but I kept my face straight. You learn to do that in sports. Never let your opponent know that you're in trouble. It just encourages him more. "No."

He was silent a moment. "Well, maybe that's for the best. Maybe you and I better talk."

"What . . . about?"

"This disk you gave Beth."

I would have liked to snatched the disk out of his hand and burned it. This wasn't supposed to be how it worked out.

"Is there someplace we can sit and talk, Robby?"

"The living room, I guess."

He followed me into the living room. There were lots of cartons still lying around, but also some chairs.

We sat down facing each other.

"I put this disk on my machine, Robby. The moment I saw what it was, I came here to return it to your father." He paused. "Which may or may not be what you wanted me to do. Right?"

I didn't answer. I was scared to answer.

"Are you trying to put your father out of business, Robby?"

I still didn't answer. I felt like a character on a TV cop show. I wanted a lawyer.

"I like your father, Robby. When Mrs. Lowenfeld got my company in the divorce settlement, it was I who recommended she get in touch with your father. I wanted to make sure my business would be in good hands. I wish Computel well. I wish your father well." He paused. He leaned forward. "Do you?"

"Yes, sir."

"So why steal from your father?"

I knew I had to tell him. I couldn't ever tell Dad. I couldn't ever tell Peg. But I knew I could and would tell him.

"I was scared, Mr. Lowenfeld."

"Of what?"

It was so hard.

"Just start at the beginning, Robby."

Start at the beginning? But where does something like this begin? And worse, where does it end?

But I told him, sitting there surrounded by boxes, him with the disk in his hand, me looking at my hands, Carol moving about in her room getting dressed, I told Mr. Lowenfeld everything . . . and it wasn't easy. I told him how scared Peggy and I were that his ex-wife was going to become our mother. (He looked startled at that.) I told him how badly I wanted to go back to Watertown, how unfair it was for Dad to move us out here. I talked about Mom and what she was like. I talked and talked and talked. I don't even know

158

if I made any sense . . . but when I was done, he just sat there looking at me.

"Thank you," he said.

I didn't know what he was thanking me for.

"You know that what you did was wrong, Robby."

"Yes, sir. I know that. I'm sorry."

"We can't program people's lives. If we could, your mom wouldn't have died. Mrs. Lowenfeld and I wouldn't have divorced. Beth wouldn't have to go back and forth between two houses. You wouldn't have had to leave Watertown and your friends. I would be a smart businessman. . . ." He smiled ruefully. "But things don't always fall the way we want them to, do they?"

They never do, I thought.

"Life isn't always fair. But we don't fight back by breaking laws and maybe hurting the very people we love most. What we have to do, and I'm doing it and your dad is doing it, everyone does it at one time or another in their lives, is . . . roll with the punches and ride out the storm. And try to make the best of a life we can't always control. And know and hope and pray that better times are coming. I don't know that there's anything else a human being can do. Do you?"

I shook my head.

He looked at me, and then held the disk out to me. "Put it back where you found it."

"It's a copy. I made it."

"Then erase it. You do that, and I'll erase it too—from my mind. And then it will be as though it never happened." He looked me right in the eye. "Is that a deal?"

I swallowed. What was there to say? He was a nice man. I felt like crying. You always cry when people are nice to you. Especially when you've been such a chump.

He stood up. "As for the soccer—" he began, and was interrupted by a voice from the front hall.

"I'm going now," Carol said. She came into the room and stopped short.

"Excuse me. I didn't know you had a visitor, Robby."

She was all dressed up. She looked very pretty. Mr. Lowenfeld stared at her.

"Do I look as familiar to you as you to me?" he said.

"As a matter of fact," Carol said with a puzzled smile, "you do."

"My name's Art Lowenfeld."

Light dawned on her face. "Of course." She laughed. "We do know each other. I'm Carol Gulden. I lived two doors down from you in West Bloomfield. I was a friend of your sister Anne's."

He laughed too. "Of course. You were Anne's best friend. The one who was such a good baseball and tennis player. But what are you doing here? In the Millers' house?"

"I just took a job here."

"A job? Here?"

"Part-time housekeeper. I've been teaching school in West Bloomfield and decided to take a year off and take some courses at the university. Where's Anne now?"

"She lives in Houston and has three kids. Wait till I tell her who I ran into."

"Speaking of which," Carol said, "what are you doing here?"

"You mean in this house?"

"Yes."

Mr. Lowenfeld glanced at me. It was like they were remembering for the first time I was in the room too.

He smiled. "I came over to invite Robby to be on our soccer team. My daughter tells me he's not very good, but I think we've got room for him anyway."

I gulped. "Thanks," I said. "I got to go."

I walked around them, but I could have walked through them and they would not have noticed. They had started talking a mile a minute about old times in West Bloomfield.

As I went up the stairs I heard him telling her that he and his wife and daughter had moved back to Michigan from California. He was working for a company here, but he really wasn't a good businessman. In fact, he'd been offered a job at the university and would start teaching in January. "A real career change," he said. "I don't think I was ever cut out to be a businessman, much to Ruth's dismay."

For a split second, I wondered if maybe that was the reason he hadn't wanted to make use of the disk.

But no, he just wasn't the type to seize an unfair edge. Even if he could profit by it. You had to admire him for that.

And then I started thinking. If he was really leaving Block Electronics, that would end his coaching baseball. Dawkins and Winkelman would be happy. Though now they'd be stuck for a sponsor and a coach.

I sat at the top of the stairs and listened to Mr. Lowenfeld and Carol talk. He went on to tell her that when they moved to Arborville, his wife had taken a job as a realtor with the Harry F. Burns Agency, and would you believe (he laughed here, but in a hurt fashion) she had fallen in love with Harry Burns, who was a *great* businessman. As an outcome of the divorce, she got the business. Burns had advised her to find someone who knew something about computers to run the business.

"And that's how come the Millers are in Arborville," he ended.

"And because the Millers are in Arborville, I got a job. And you and I met again?"

"It *is* a small world when all is said and done. Tell me, Carol . . . are you . . . did you . . . ."

"Am I married?"

"Yes."

"No. I never got married. I'm sorry to say that I'm as free as the proverbial bird."

"Well, would one free bird like to have dinner tonight with another free bird?"

"I'd love to," Carol said.

That was all. I sat at the top of the stairs and listened to them falling in love, 'cause that was exactly what was happening. Then I went into Dad's study and erased the disk and put it back in his file.

When I was done, they were gone. About an hour later Peggy and Dad got back. They'd seen some nice furniture but hadn't bought any because Peggy wanted Carol's opinion too. Which annoyed Dad. He was getting tired of her matchmaking.

I told Peggy that she wasn't gonna get Carol's opinion about furniture because "she's gone off to have dinner with Mr. Lowenfeld."

When they looked astonished, I told them what had happened. Not all. Naturally, I left out the part about my copying Dad's disk. I told them that Mr. Lowenfeld had come over to ask me to be on the soccer team (which he said he had) and that he and Carol had turned out to be old friends (which they had). And tonight the two of them were having dinner together.

"That's wonderful," Dad said, and meant it.

Peggy looked sick.

"Hey," I said to her later when we were alone, "you don't have to matchmake Dad and Carol, because Mrs. Lowenfeld is probably gonna marry her boss—Harry F. Burns."

"How do you know this?"

"I heard him tell Carol that. I don't think even Beth knows it. Anyway, nothing's going to happen to Dad

163

or to us. Your plan's kaput, and so's mine. The really bad part is that now we're not gonna make it back to Watertown."

Peggy shook her head. "I don't care about going back to Watertown as long as Dad doesn't marry Mrs. Lowenfeld. There's some really neat shopping centers in this town, Robby. And I bet I can find someone else beside Carol for Dad to marry."

I just shook my head. What could you do about her? She'd fallen in love with matchmaking.

That afternoon we went back to the Lowenfelds' for dinner. And there was a jovial fat man with a cigar there, and his name was Harry F. Burns.

"Warren, Peggy, Robby, I'd like you to meet my boss, Harry Burns. I told you this was going to be a special dinner, and this is why. I've told Beth, and now I want to tell the whole world. Harry and I are going to be married this fall."

Hardly news to me and Peg. Though we pretended polite surprise. What was really new and different though was Mrs. Lowenfeld. She seemed genuinely relaxed for the first time. She laughed. She didn't seem so organized and coordinated. She was happy. Beth looked pretty glum though. I wanted to tell her it was all going to be okay. To roll with the punches and ride out the storm because, though she didn't know it yet, she might be getting the world's greatest stepmother in Carol. The greatest backup Mom ever.

As for Dad. Our Dad. If he was hurt, he didn't show it. He congratulated both Mrs. Lowenfeld and Mr.

Burns. Mr. Burns was a funny man. He made a lot of jokes. Some of them you could even laugh at without being just polite.

After dinner Beth and I went down to play Ping-Pong again.

"I'm sorry about your folks not going to get together again."

"I'm sorry you're not gonna get back to Watertown."

"I am too. But my friend Monk Kelly's gonna come out here for a football game. I'll introduce you to him. You'll like him. You're a lot like him."

"Yeah? What's that supposed to mean?"

"Hey, he's my best friend. That's what it means."

That was as close as I was gonna come to telling her that I'd like to be friends with her.

She got the point. "Okay," she said, and grinned, and slammed a ball by me.

Well, my story really ends here. Everything else has nothing to do with us. People are getting married or falling in love or both.

Some good is going to come out of this move to Michigan though. Computel is going to sponsor our baseball team in the spring. And Carol's said she's willing to coach us. Mr. Lowenfeld'll be too busy getting adjusted to his new career. That'll be something, having an experienced and competitive woman coach.

Peggy's stopped feeling sad about Carol not marrying Dad. Somehow she's found out that Arborville,

Michigan, has the highest rate of single women in this state, and she's sure she can find one for Dad.

"You ought to cut that out," I told her. "It doesn't work."

"What doesn't work?"

"Scheming for adults. Trying to program people's lives."

"Where'd you learn to talk that way, little brother?"

I blushed. "Never mind. I just know."

I spoke so convincingly that I know she believed me and would have stopped matchmaking, except that one night Carol invited Mr. Lowenfeld for dinner. At our big old round table they talked about how they used to know each other as kids and how wonderful it was to rediscover each other as adults. Dad said, "This sounds serious."

"It is," Mr. Lowenfeld said, and Carol blushed.

"And you know, Warren," Mr. Lowenfeld added with just the faintest twinkle in his eye, "I've really got Robby to thank for this."

My heart stood still.

"He engineered the whole thing."

"You mean by trying out for the soccer team that morning?" Dad asked.

Mr. Lowenfeld winked at me ever so slightly. "That's right."

Peggy was furious. "Did you really bring him and Carol together?" she asked me later that evening.

I shook my head. There was no way I could explain to her what had really happened. There was no way

I could explain it to anyone. Well, I've learned two great lessons from this. The first is: Don't break laws. The second is: Don't try to run your folks' lives—or anyone's life for that matter. It won't work.

Peggy hasn't learned that second lesson though. Just yesterday she came home from school with the news that her social studies teacher, Miss Scott, isn't married and that she is pretty and supposed to be a good cook.

"Teachers don't make a lot of money," Peg said, "so I thought I'd ask her if she'd also like a part-time job as a housekeeper after Carol leaves."

I groaned. Dad sighed. But old Peg's going to ask her. I'll let you know how it comes out.